"I want my ring without delay."

Lang took her hand as he continued, "So what's your answer? Are you going to marry me?"

Cassandra snatched her hand away. "I don't understand *why* you want to marry me.... And *don't* mention sex...."

Blue eyes laughing, he said, "I wouldn't dare."

"I'm sure there are dozens of women who would be prepared to keep you happy in bed."

"Oh, I'm sure you're right. But I don't want a succession of bed partners. I want a wife."

LEE WILKINSON lives with her husband in a three-hundred-year-old stone cottage in a village in Derbyshire, England. Most winters they get cut off by snow! Both enjoy traveling, and previously joined forces with their daughter and son-in-law, spending a year going around the world "on a shoestring" while their son looked after Kelly, their much-loved German shepherd dog. Lee's hobbies are reading and gardening and holding impromptu barbecues for her long-suffering family and friends.

Books by Lee Wilkinson

HARLEQUIN PRESENTS®
1933—THE SECRET MOTHER
1991—A HUSBAND'S REVENGE
2024—WEDDING FEVER
2090—MARRIAGE ON TRIAL

Don't miss any of our special offers. Write to us at the following address for information on our newest releases.

Harlequin Reader Service
U.S.: 3010 Walden Ave., P.O. Box 1325, Buffalo, NY 14269
Canadian: P.O. Box 609, Fort Erie, Ont. L2A 5X3

Lee Wilkinson

THE MARRIAGE TAKEOVER

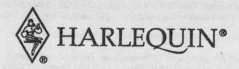

TORONTO • NEW YORK • LONDON
AMSTERDAM • PARIS • SYDNEY • HAMBURG
STOCKHOLM • ATHENS • TOKYO • MILAN • MADRID
PRAGUE • WARSAW • BUDAPEST • AUCKLAND

ISBN 0-373-12107-5

THE MARRIAGE TAKEOVER

First North American Publication 2000.

Visit us at www.eHarlequin.com

Printed in U.S.A.

CHAPTER ONE

LANG DALTON'S silver-grey, chauffeur-driven limousine had been waiting for them at San Francisco International Airport. Ensconced in the purring luxury, Cassandra Vallance sighed and glanced at the dark-haired, good-looking man by her side.

In response to the apprehension in that glance, Alan Brent took the hand that was wearing his diamond cluster, and patted it with a there-there gesture that was meant to calm and comfort.

Safely cut off from the driver by a glass partition, he said, 'I know this weekend was sprung on us, but try to relax, darling. Lang Dalton may be a multi-millionaire and the Great I Am, but there's really nothing to worry about.'

'I know so little about him. Has he a wife?'

'Yes, he married a woman the media once described as "America's most beautiful socialite". I gather she comes from one of California's top families, the kind who hobnob with film stars and presidents.'

'Have they been married long?'

'About a couple of years.'

'Does he know we're getting married?'

'Yes. I told him myself. Though I probably didn't need to. He seems au fait with everything that goes on. Where he gets all his information is a mystery.'

'How well do you know him?'

'Although I've been working for him for over four years, I've only met him once,' Alan told her. 'That was about eighteen months ago when he came over to England.'

5

'What's he like?' The question came in a rush. Until now, for some odd, unaccountable reason, she had been loath to ask.

'Hard, autocratic, ruthless, a bit of a cold fish, just as his reputation suggests. Not the kind of man to get on the wrong side of.

'Most people seem to be a bit in awe of him. There was a story going around that even his own PA was afraid of him...

'But, on the plus side, he's known to have firm principles, to care for the environment, and to be both honest and scrupulously fair, even generous.'

Seeing she still looked far from happy, Alan added, 'So what if he is something of a despot? He can't eat us.'

'That's what I keep telling myself, but my instincts won't buy it. I feel...'

She came to a halt and glanced away, unable to tell him exactly what she did feel. Coming from a woman who was regarded as being intelligent, efficient and level-headed, it would sound ridiculous to say, 'I have a kind of foreboding. A premonition that something disastrous is going to happen and my life will never be the same again.'

His eyes resting on her lovely profile, Alan pressed, 'How *do* you feel?'

'Threatened,' she confessed.

'Oh, come on!' He laughed, unable to understand her fears. 'Lang Dalton isn't an absolute ogre... And it's not like you to be so melodramatic.'

'I don't know what's come over me,' she admitted. 'But I can't get it out of my head that nothing's going to go right.'

His brown eyes growing impatient, Alan urged, 'Think positive. All you have to do is take care not to get on the wrong side of him...'

She bit her lip, knowing quite well this feeling of being threatened wasn't rational, but unable to dismiss it.

'Look at it this way: in the unlikely event of you incurring his dislike or disapproval, the worst he can do is dispense with your services. I'd hate to part with you, you're the best PA I've ever had, but it wouldn't be the end of the world.

'Now for goodness' sake stop worrying and enjoy the chance to see something of California. The Big Sur is one of the most scenic stretches of coastline anywhere in the world, and when we head south we'll have an ideal opportunity to see it from the air.'

When she said nothing, Alan added, 'We're really very lucky. This kind of social get-together is unprecedented. Usually Dalton keeps his business affairs and his private life totally separate.'

'Which makes me wonder what prompted this particular invitation,' she remarked uneasily.

Knowing they hadn't been so much invited as summoned, Alan shrugged. 'Presumably it's a new policy.'

'I still can't understand why he insisted that I should accompany you.'

'Perhaps it was a question of numbers. We'll be joining a kind of small house party, I gather. And he didn't exactly insist…'

But Lang Dalton had ordered arbitrarily, 'I want you to come over to San Francisco for a long weekend and bring Miss Vallance with you.'

Alan sighed inwardly. Knowing that Cassandra had always wanted to travel, he'd presumed she would be pleased. Only as they'd reached their destination had he realized that, for some reason he still couldn't fathom, she felt quite the opposite.

'Look, darling, I'm sorry you're so averse to the whole thing, but it would have been difficult to refuse…'

With his entire future depending on not crossing Lang

Dalton, it would have been suicidal, and Cassandra knew it.

She was proud of Alan who, at only twenty-five, was head of Finance at the London offices of Dalton International, and had a brilliant career predicted for him.

'And it's only for four days,' he added, no longer trying to hide his exasperation.

'Yes, I know. I'm sorry. I'm behaving like a perfect idiot.' She smiled, a smile that lit her green eyes and brought her heart-shaped face to glowing life. 'Please forget all I've said and let's make the most of the weekend.'

'That's my girl.'

As he finished speaking, the limousine drew up outside the twin towers of the glass and concrete building that housed Dalton International.

Almost before the chauffeur had opened the car door, a brisk young man appeared to greet them. Having taken charge of their luggage, he escorted them up in the high-speed elevator to the bright, baking heat of the roof, where a helicopter was waiting on the pad.

Moments later, rotor-blades whirling, they lifted off into the sun-filled dome of a cloudless blue sky, the spectacular skyline of downtown San Francisco falling away beneath them. Cassandra could only admire the meticulous efficiency of the whole operation.

After a breathtaking flight down the rugged coast, they turned inland and headed for the Sierra Roca, where Lang Dalton had his home. The superb scenery became sun-baked and mountainous, and the conclusion of their journey proved to be equally impressive.

Once again a sleek limousine was standing by to ferry them the short distance from the landing-pad to a white, one-storey, Spanish-style hacienda.

Built around a huge central patio and swimming pool,

it was surrounded by extensive gardens, archways, bou-
gainvillaea-draped terraces, fountains and statuary.

From the air the lavish spread had looked like a film
set, the very epitome of where the wealthy and privi-
leged lived.

When the big car slid to a halt on the paved apron
outside the main entrance, their uniformed chauffeur
jumped out and opened the door. Almost before they had
time to get out, a white-coated servant appeared and
whisked away their small amount of luggage.

At the same instant a tall, wide-shouldered man with
thick, sun-bleached fair hair appeared on the terrace and
came down the shallow flight of steps to meet them.

His clothes were casual: well-cut olive-green trousers
and a silk, open-necked shirt. He looked completely assured and coolly elegant.

'Brent...' He shook hands with Alan, and turned to
look at Cassandra.

She saw his face was lean and tanned with thickly
lashed, heavy-lidded eyes, and a strong, bony nose. He
was about thirty-two or three, she judged, much better
looking than she had imagined, and even more formidable.

'Miss Vallance...' There was a ghost of a polite smile
around his mouth, but it didn't reach his eyes. 'I'm Lang
Dalton...'

Very conscious of the way he dwarfed her five feet
seven inches, and of the mature width of his shoulders,
she murmured a formal, 'How do you do?'

'Welcome to the Villa San Gabriel. I hope you had a
good flight?' His voice was attractive and unexpectedly
cultured, his speech clipped and decisive.

His hand, well-shaped and muscular, closed over hers,
and she felt a rising panic as he looked her over from
head to toe, coolly appraising.

She was dressed in a businesslike grey silk suit and
her ash-brown hair had been tamed into an elegant coil

which emphasized her long, slender neck, her high cheekbones, and the pure line of her jaw.

With that wonderful bone-structure she could have been part Cherokee, he thought. Her winged brows and slightly slanting green eyes, her wide, generous mouth and cleft chin made her one of the most unusually beautiful women he'd ever seen.

Seeing she was made uncomfortable by his silent scrutiny, he said, 'I decided it was high time I met you.'

'I'm surprised you even knew of my existence.' Her husky voice, and the way she withdrew her hand, betrayed her nervousness.

'I make it my business to know about the people who work for me.'

But surely he couldn't know about all the people in such a vast organization? She felt afraid. Singled out. Like a victim chosen to be sacrificed.

Abruptly, he said, 'You're not at all as I'd...' There was a fleeting pause before he added, 'Pictured.'

'Neither are you.' The imprudent words were out before she could stop them.

'Oh? What had you expected?'

Someone short and paunchy, thick-necked and balding, with an aggressive, belligerent manner, rather than this air of contained but absolute authority.

But she could hardly tell him that. 'I—I hadn't realized you'd be quite so young.'

A strange inflection in his voice, he said slowly, 'And I hadn't realized you'd be quite so beautiful.'

As he spoke she saw that his teeth were excellent, his mouth wide and firm, the upper lip thinner than the lower... A controlled mouth, she thought, yet it held a disturbing touch of sensuality. Despite the hot sun, a strange shiver ran through her.

He noticed that betraying movement, and eyes that were a deep blue with darker rims to the irises caught and held hers.

Possibly he read the apprehension in their green depths, because he asked silkily, 'Are you afraid of me, Miss Vallance?'

'Aren't most people?'

Even as she regretted her unthinking retort, she recalled Alan saying, 'There was a story going around that even his own PA was afraid of him...'

If she had let it pass casually he might have taken the remark at face value, but, only too aware of her blunder, she found herself flushing furiously.

A white line appeared round his mouth. 'I see you've been listening to some old gossip.'

There was a frozen silence, then Alan, who had been standing by unheeded and forgotten, stepped forward and, giving her a warning look, began hastily, 'I'm sure Cass didn't mean—'

'Perhaps you'll allow Miss Vallance to speak for herself,' Lang Dalton broke in curtly.

Cassandra lifted her chin and looked him in the face. His grim expression told her that any attempt at an explanation could only make matters worse.

'I'm sorry,' she said quietly. 'I shouldn't have said what I did.'

'Even if it were true?'

'Especially if it were true.' By her side, she felt Alan stiffen, and wondered despairingly why she, who was normally prudent and diplomatic, seemed hell-bent on signing her own death warrant.

Trembling a little, she waited for the axe to fall.

Instead, the anger in the dark blue eyes changed to ironic amusement. 'I see you have a sense of humour.'

'A sense of self-preservation might be more use.'

He laughed, white teeth gleaming against his tan. 'I thought perhaps you liked to live dangerously?'

She shook her head. 'I'm not the type. Too chicken.'

'Somehow I doubt it. But I'll be able to judge for myself when I get to know you better...' There was a lot about this woman he still didn't know. But he fully intended to.

Disconcerted by the steely purpose she sensed beneath the mundane words, she glanced at Alan, who, excluded from the conversation, moved a little restlessly.

Lang Dalton's gaze flicked to him, and then back to Cassandra. 'In the meantime, I expect you'd like to have a shower and get settled in before dinner?' He lifted a hand.

A Mexican houseboy in white baggy trousers and a tunic appeared as if by magic.

'Manuel will show you both to your rooms.'

'Thank you.' With a feeling of reprieve, Cassandra turned and followed the short, slim youth up the steps and across the wide terrace, conscious that Lang Dalton stood quite still where he was and watched them.

When they were well out of earshot, Alan remarked, 'Well, it could have been worse, I suppose... And presumably there'll be other people present from now on. It won't be just the two of us in the hot seat...'

But it hadn't been the two of them. After that first handshake, Lang Dalton had virtually ignored Alan's presence and singled her out in a way that had totally unnerved her.

'And, in spite of getting off to an unfortunate start, he seemed to like you.'

No, Lang Dalton hadn't liked her; Cassandra was certain of that. Something had made her of interest to him. Something, intuition told her, that would disturb her, if she knew what it was.

Her sense of fear and foreboding had, if anything, increased rather than lessened. She felt like someone standing blindfold on a narrow ledge at the top of a precipice, only too aware of the danger, but without a clue how she got there or how to save herself.

The houseboy led them through an impressive,

creeper-hung doorway and into the cool interior of the villa.

They were surprised to find themselves in a kind of large atrium, with a roof open to the rafters, and a series of wide archways that led off in various directions.

To the left, on slightly different levels, was a spacious living and dining area. Plain white walls, terrazzo floors, green plants, and the minimum of furniture, made it pleasant and restful, while one or two dramatic, abstract paintings added life and colour.

Clearly it was the home of a couple who liked their living to be stylish and uncluttered.

'This way, *señor*, *señorita*...' At the end of a wide corridor the houseboy opened a door to the left. 'This is your room, *señor*.' Then to Cassandra, 'If you will follow me, *señorita*... Your room is along this way.'

For some reason she had expected them to have adjoining rooms, and her heart sank. Giving Alan a rather uncertain smile, she turned and obediently followed the youth.

By the time she had been shown to a room on the opposite side of the house, Cassandra had realized that she was about as far away from her fiancé as it was possible to be.

Was that a deliberate policy? she wondered. Or was it simply that the closer rooms had already been allotted to other guests?

There had been no sign of anyone else, apart from the servants and Lang Dalton himself, but perhaps they hadn't arrived yet, or were taking a siesta?

Her room, with its pastel-coloured walls, off-white carpet and draped muslin curtains, was delightfully cool and spacious. Her luggage had been placed on an old Spanish chest.

The outer wall was a series of arches, each with sliding glass panels which opened on to the central patio and pool. With its blue water and palm trees, its colourful loungers and umbrella-shaded tables, it looked extremely enticing, but was totally deserted.

For a moment she was tempted to find the swimsuit Alan had suggested she pack. But, as a guest, she could hardly use the pool without being invited to.

Instead she would take a shower. There was a sumptuous *en-suite* bathroom, with a frosted-glass shower stall, lots of mirrors, and a large sunken tub with steps leading down.

It was a far cry from the poky little bathroom she shared with Penny—once her room-mate at college, now her flatmate—where the bath was watermarked, the shower dripped, and one small, spotted mirror was hung a foot too low. Imagining her friend swooning at so much sensuous luxury made her smile.

Hearing about the proposed trip to California, and shrewdly noting Cassandra's reaction to it, Penny had exclaimed, 'And this is so awful? I thought you'd always wanted to travel? Believe me, I'd give my eye-teeth to be in your shoes. I practically swoon at the *thought* of staying with a millionaire...'

Then, with a snort of disgust, she'd said, 'Some people—naming no names, but follow my eyes—just don't appreciate how lucky they are!'

Cheered by the thought of the other girl, Cassandra unpacked and put away her clothes, leaving out fresh undies and a simple silk sheath in subtle shades of turquoise, green and gold.

Showered and dressed, she had just brushed her hair and was about to take it up into its usual coil, when there was a discreet tap at the door.

So Alan had managed to track her down.

A smile on her lips, she hurried to open it, and found the houseboy hovering.

'Señor Dalton asks that you will join him for a predinner drink.'

Scarcely ready, she hesitated. 'At once?'

'*Sí, señorita.*'

Knowing it would be unwise to keep him waiting, she braced herself and, leaving her hair curling loosely on her shoulders, closed her door and followed the slight figure.

Through the open windows she could faintly hear what sounded like one of the gardeners at work with a lawn mower. Apart from that, and the splash of an unseen fountain, it was almost eerily quiet, and there was still no sign of a soul.

When they reached the living area, the houseboy informed her, 'Señor Dalton is on the terrace.'

'Thank you, Manuel.'

He gave her a shy smile and departed, soft-footed.

The sliding glass opened on to a secluded terrace roofed with vines and screened from the pool and patio by a white, wrought-iron grille.

There was some comfortable-looking outdoor furniture scattered about, and a small but well-stocked refrigerated bar at one end.

Lang Dalton, who was lounging in a fan-backed wicker chair, rose to his feet at her approach and came to meet her.

She had been praying that his wife would be there, that other guests would be present, but he was alone.

Wearing a white evening shirt, a black bow-tie and a lightweight dinner-jacket, he looked both handsome and charismatic.

Taking her hand in a formal gesture, he said, 'I must apologize if I've rushed you?'

'No, not at all,' she murmured, hoping he hadn't noticed her stiffen at his touch.

Still holding her hand, he queried, 'Are you happy with your room?'

'Very happy, thank you... And Cleopatra herself would have approved of the bathing facilities.'

His eyes amused, he said, 'I doubt it. We're fresh out of asses' milk.'

Made uncomfortable by his maleness, his undeniable and unexpected attraction, she withdrew her hand, and asked as lightly as possible, 'Where is everyone?'

'*Everyone* being…?'

'Well…the rest of your guests.'

She saw his firm lips twitch.

The knowledge that her reference to other guests had appealed to his sense of humour made her add uneasily, 'Alan said something about there being a small house party.'

'In the event, I changed my mind,' Lang Dalton told her smoothly. 'There are no other guests.'

Feeling as though the ground had been cut from under her feet, she said blankly, 'Oh.'

'I hope you're not too disappointed?'

The gleam in his eye made it clear that he knew how she felt and was enjoying her discomfort.

Recovering her equilibrium, she schooled her expression into an untroubled mask, and answered, 'No, not at all. Who was it said "Fewer people can only be an advantage"?'

'Bravo!'

She got the distinct impression that he was applauding her performance more than the sentiments.

His glance moved from her face to the tumble of silky hair, and, lifting his hand, he picked up a loose tendril and straightened it before letting it spring back. 'Naturally curly?'

'Yes,' she said in a stifled voice.

Alan had made no mention of Lang Dalton being a philanderer, so perhaps his intention had merely been to tip her off balance once more.

If so, he'd succeeded.

Head tilted a little to one side, he studied her. 'With

your hair down, you look delightfully young and innocent.'

Though the words were flattering, she felt oddly convinced that no compliment had been intended. In fact his appraisal bordered on the critical, and, wondering if he found her appearance too casual for his liking, she began a shade defensively, 'Well, I usually take it up, but I...'

'But you didn't have enough time...' He ran the tips of his fingers lightly down one cheek, making her shiver. 'And you're not wearing any make-up. Dear me, in spite of your tactful denial, I *must* have rushed you.'

It was a moment or two before she managed to say jerkily, 'In this kind of heat I prefer not to wear any make-up.'

'Truth, or discretion?' he queried, his smile openly mocking.

'Truth.' With well-marked brows and lashes, and a flawless skin, she didn't really need make-up.

'Sit down, Miss Vallance.' He indicated a chair next to his own. 'Or may I call you Cassandra?'

'Please do,' she agreed with distant civility, and sat down with the greatest reluctance. Oh, why wasn't his wife here?

'What would you like to drink, Cassandra?'

'Something long and cold and not too alcoholic, please.'

Seeing him lift a blond brow, she added, 'I still feel a little dehydrated from the flight.'

'Then we'll make it a very weak margarita.' Crossing to the bar, he rimmed two glasses with salt and poured crushed ice into a cocktail shaker, before asking, 'Do you like flying?'

Wondering where on earth Alan had got to, she answered abstractedly, 'I haven't done a great deal.'

'How much have you done?'

Lang Dalton, it seemed, didn't care for any kind of evasion.

'Just one trip to Paris,' she said evenly. 'This is the first time I've flown long-haul.'

'And you didn't like it?'

'Yes, I liked it.'

'But you didn't want to come to California?'

Startled, she asked, 'What makes you think that?'

'It's quite obvious.'

'Really, you're mistaken,' she protested.

'Don't lie to me,' he said shortly, and wondered, Had she any idea who he was? 'Why didn't you want to come?'

She racked her brains to find some diplomatic excuse that would sound feasible, but her mind stayed a blank, and finally she admitted, 'I—I don't know. There was no real reason.'

Aware that what he saw as her refusal to answer had vexed him, she added helplessly, 'I just had a strange feeling that things weren't going to go smoothly, and...' The words tailed off.

Careful not to look in his direction, she heard the rhythmic shush of the cocktail shaker, then the sound of its contents being poured.

A moment or two later he put a tall, chilled glass into her hand and, taking his seat beside her, prompted, 'And?'

'And they didn't... You and I got off on the wrong foot.'

'Correction,' he said softly. '*You* got off on the wrong foot.'

She forced herself to meet his eyes. 'Yes, I suppose so. I'm sorry about that.'

He made no comment, and after a moment she looked away uncomfortably.

While they sipped their drinks, she was aware that his gaze never left her face. Flustered by that relentless scrutiny, she tried to think of something to say, while the silence stretched unbearably.

At length, in desperation, she blurted out, 'I can't imagine where Alan's got to.'

'If I'd wanted Brent here, I would have sent for him,' Lang informed her crisply. 'It was you I wanted to talk to. You have a lovely voice, so use it. Tell me about yourself.'

Strangely unwilling, as though telling this man about herself would somehow make her vulnerable, she began, 'Well, I came to work for Dalton International when—'

'I'm not asking about the business side,' he broke in with a touch of impatience. 'It's *you* I want to know about. How old are you?'

Reminding herself that he was her boss as well as Alan's, she replied stiffly, 'Twenty-two.'

'Where do you live?'

'In Bayswater.'

'Alone?'

'I share a flat.'

'With Brent?'

'With a girlfriend.'

'Where were you born?'

'Oxford.'

'Have you any brothers or sisters?'

'No, I was an only child.' She was answering each question with studied politeness, but making very little effort to elaborate.

His annoyance barely masked, he said peremptorily, 'I would prefer you to tell me in your own words rather than make it into an interrogation.'

Allowing a few seconds for that to sink in, he added, 'Suppose you start with your home background—parents, schooling, that kind of thing.'

'My father was a historian, an academic who lived in Chaucer's time rather than in the real world. My mother was a career woman, and ran a successful secretarial agency. They were both in their late thirties and set in their ways before I was born.'

Making no comment, his eyes on her face, he waited.

Flatly, dispassionately, she went on, 'Because neither of them wanted, or had any time for, a child, they hired a nanny until I was old enough to be sent away to boarding-school.'

An expression she couldn't decipher crossed his face, before he asked, 'Were you happy there?'

'Most of the time.' Except when holidays came round. Then, because it wasn't 'convenient' to have her home, her parents had farmed her out to various distant relatives, until she'd been old enough to make her own plans.

'And when you left school?'

'I went to college.'

In response to his little frown of irritation, she continued, 'When I graduated last year, I was offered a job at Dalton International, and I've been Alan's secretary and personal assistant for the past five months.'

Her left hand was lightly gripping the arm of her chair, and, noticing Lang Dalton's glance linger on her engagement ring, she found herself wondering whether he questioned Alan's motives for giving her the job.

Lifting her chin, she asked, 'But perhaps you think I wasn't experienced enough to have been offered such a post?'

'I don't think anything of the kind. When Brent made you his PA, he was acting on my instructions.'

Cassandra's green eyes widened. She'd had absolutely no idea. Alan hadn't breathed a word.

'Surprised?' Lang Dalton didn't miss a thing.

'Yes,' she admitted. Then, with an odd little shiver, she began, 'Why did you—?'

He cut her short. 'I knew you had all the necessary qualifications.'

So had several other people who had been with Dalton's a great deal longer.

Cassandra had presumed at the time that it was Alan's

decision. He'd been taking her out for several weeks, and, afraid there might be strings attached, she had thought long and hard before accepting.

Watching her transparent face, Lang asked, 'What's Brent like to work for?'

Alan had turned out to be a very good boss, and working for him had proved a pleasure.

She said as much, and watched Lang Dalton smile sardonically.

'You think I'm prejudiced?'

'Aren't you?'

'No,' she denied hardly. 'I'm sure anyone else would tell you the same.'

'Your loyalty does you credit.'

Refusing to protest further, she bit her lip and said nothing.

'When did you two get engaged?'

'About three months ago.'

'And you're planning to get married...when?'

'In just over a week.'

'I had the impression it was next spring.'

'We brought the date forward.'

'Any particular reason?' he asked idly.

Flushing furiously, she said in a half-strangled voice, 'I'm not pregnant, Mr Dalton, if that's what you mean,' and watched the build-up of tension in his big frame relax.

'Forgive me,' he said smoothly, 'but there's always a possibility, and it might have affected my future plans for the pair of you.'

Taken aback, she asked, 'What kind of future plans?'

Ignoring the question, he asked abruptly, 'Do you love Brent?'

Her private feelings had nothing whatsoever to do with this arrogant man, and for a moment she was sorely tempted to jump up and walk away. But, knowing any open discourtesy on her part might rebound on Alan, she hesitated.

The dark blue eyes pinned her. 'You obviously feel that I've no right to be asking such personal questions.'

Meeting his gaze steadily, she said, 'I really can't see that they're relevant.'

'Brent is poised to go to the top in my organization, and a top executive's working life is invariably affected by his or her private life.

'I've found from past experience that it's almost impossible to separate the two. So before I promote anyone I feel justified in asking enough questions to size up the situation...'

So that was why they had both been invited. What he'd meant by future plans.

'It's up to you, of course. You don't have to answer.'

But if she didn't it would no doubt adversely affect Alan's prospects.

Biting back her resentment, she said, 'I love him very much. I wouldn't be marrying him if I didn't.'

His blue eyes cynical, Lang observed, 'In my experience, women marry men for a variety of reasons, and love isn't necessarily one of them.'

'You seem to have been...' She stopped speaking abruptly.

'Do go on,' he said silkily. 'What do I seem to have been?'

'Unfortunate in your experience of women.'

The instant the fatal sentence was spoken, she could have bitten her tongue. He looked absolutely *livid*.

As though the words echoed inside her head, she could hear Alan saying, 'All you have to do is take care not to get on the wrong side of him.'

Her heart like lead, she realized that though they had only been here a matter of hours she'd managed to do just that.

After a moment or two, his anger under control, his

hard face devoid of expression, he asked brusquely, 'So what exactly have you heard?'

'I—I don't know what you mean.' She was genuinely at a loss.

His eyes holding hers, he said slowly, 'I could almost believe that.'

'You can believe it, Mr Dalton. It's the truth.'

'Do you mean there isn't any gossip going the rounds? Or you don't listen to it?'

'If you mean gossip about *you*, so far as I know there isn't any.'

'That's surprising. Though at this end every effort was made to curb it, it's almost impossible to stamp it out altogether. You'd heard the old rumour that my PA was afraid of me...'

Not knowing what to say, Cassandra stayed silent.

'And your remark just now suggested you'd heard...other things.'

Shaking her head, she chose her words with care. 'I said what I did because I thought you sounded... somewhat disillusioned... Obviously I got the wrong impression.'

Then, in a rush, she said, 'I'm sorry. I know you're angry with me, but please don't hold it against Alan.'

Lang's dark blue gaze narrowed on her face. Mockingly, he said, 'I could almost believe you *do* love him.'

Watching her bite her lip, he smiled thinly.

Afraid to speak in case she put her foot in it again, she twisted her hands together in her lap and prayed that someone would come and break up this most uncomfortable tête-à-tête.

CHAPTER TWO

HER prayer was answered.

'So there you are, Cass…'

The familiar voice sent a flood of relief surging through her, and she looked up eagerly to see Alan crossing the terrace.

Freshly showered and shaved, his evening jacket immaculate, his dark hair expertly styled, he looked every inch the rising young executive.

Sounding more than a little put out, he added, 'I've been waiting for you.'

'Come and join us,' Lang Dalton invited blandly, his air now that of a civil host. 'What will you have to drink?'

'Sweet vermouth, please, with ice and lemon.'

Rising to his feet, Lang queried, 'Would you like a refill, Cassandra?'

Catching Alan's flicker of surprise at the use of her Christian name, she answered awkwardly, 'No, thank you. As a rule I don't drink at all.'

When the tall figure had crossed to the bar, Alan came and sat down opposite her. His good-looking face aggrieved, he complained, 'I hung about for what seemed an age… In the end I was forced to ask the houseboy where your room was.'

Seeing his dignity had been wounded, she began, 'I'm sorry, I—'

But he was going on, 'When I found it was empty, and there was no sign of you, I began to wonder where the devil you'd got to.'

'I'm sorry,' she said again, 'but I—'

She broke off as, having passed Alan his vermouth, Lang Dalton came and sat down again beside her.

'There's no need for Cassandra to apologize,' he said coolly, obviously having overheard the low-toned conversation. 'The fault was mine. I asked her to have a private drink with me...'

Alan looked startled.

'I wanted to sound her out about something before I spoke to you. In the event I didn't get round to it.'

His brown eyes holding a hint of anxiety, Alan asked, 'What did you want to speak to me about?'

'As we'll be dining shortly, I'd prefer to leave any business discussions until later,' Lang Dalton told him. He continued decidedly, 'I make it a rule never to talk shop at the table—whether or not there are other guests present.'

As though picking up a cue, Alan remarked, 'I haven't seen any of the other guests around... But perhaps they're not arriving until tomorrow?'

'On this occasion there are no other guests. I decided to dispense with the social side and concentrate on the business in hand.'

As he finished speaking, Manuel appeared and announced that dinner was served.

'Shall we go in?' Lang got to his feet and waited courteously for Cassandra to lead the way.

The long, polished dining table looked a picture, with fine napkins, cut glass, and a centre-piece of fresh flowers.

It was set for three.

As their host moved to the head of the table and seated Cassandra on his right, Alan queried politely, 'Your wife isn't dining with us?'

Lang glanced at him and, the muscles in his jaw tightening, made no reply.

Obviously nonplussed by the other man's silence,

Alan pursued, 'Perhaps we'll have the pleasure of meeting her tomorrow?'

'That isn't likely.' His expression a mixture of cold fury and naked pain, Lang added curtly, 'My wife died nearly six months ago. Surely you knew that?'

Thrown into confusion, Alan stammered, 'N-no... I— I'm sorry... I had no idea.'

Sitting still and silent, Cassandra could only feel bitterly sorry for him, and angry that Lang Dalton had allowed him to make such a blunder.

A black-coated butler appeared and began to serve melon boats with a compote of chilled summer fruits.

In a strained silence, and never having felt less like eating, she picked up her spoon and began to eat. After a while, glancing up unwarily, she encountered her host's intent gaze.

Cassandra's eyes instantly dropped, but not before he'd read in them anger and resentment and an unspoken accusation.

Speaking expressly to her, as though Alan weren't even present, he said with a hint of steel, 'You appear to blame me for the...er...*faux pas*?'

Refusing to be intimidated, she answered quietly, 'I do.'

'Well, that's honest, if not particularly prudent. May I enquire why?'

Knowing she had nothing to lose, she lifted her chin and looked him in the eye. 'While we were on our way here I asked Alan what you were like...'

Without looking at him she was aware that Alan was sitting transfixed, while, one blond brow raised, Lang waited.

'He said you were known to have principles, and to be scrupulously fair... If that's true, I think you'll admit it would have been rather more ethical on your part, and prevented any such mistake, if you'd mentioned your wife's death earlier.'

There was dead silence for perhaps ten seconds, before Lang Dalton admitted soberly, 'You're quite right,
of course.'

Turning to Alan, he added, 'Please accept my apolo-
gies. At first I presumed that it wasn't a genuine blunder,
merely a rather clumsy attempt to conceal the fact that
you knew about Nina's death and the circumstances.'

Then to Cassandra he said, 'In my own defence I must
say that in spite of strenuous efforts to keep things
hushed up I could hardly believe the story hadn't leaked
out...'

He stopped speaking as a maid appeared and began
to clear away the dishes, while the butler produced the
next course.

Lang Dalton was a surprising man, Cassandra
thought; despite his arbitrary manner and his undoubted
arrogance, he'd been big enough not only to admit a
fault, but to apologize.

And clearly Alan's assessment of him as being hard
and lacking in emotion was a false one. Judging by that
look of stark pain, he'd loved his wife very much, and
was still devastated by her death.

Nina—he'd called her Nina—must have been quite
young, much too young to die, and in what appeared to
have been tragic and singular circumstances.

Circumstances that had obviously caused tongues to
wag. From Lang Dalton's reaction it seemed clear that
he'd been the victim of some vicious gossip, which had
left him angry and embittered, suspicious of the most
innocent remark.

She could only feel sorry for him.

Having served them from a seafood platter and filled
the long-stemmed glasses with a fine white wine from
the Napa Valley, at a nod from his master, the butler
departed.

When they were once more alone, their host remarked
a shade drily, 'Now, as I've made light conversation

virtually impossible, I think I'll break my own rule and get down to business, and the reason I invited you both here.

'George Irvine, who worked for my father before me, is retiring at the end of next month, so I need a new head of West Coast Finances…'

Looking as if he couldn't believe his ears, Alan echoed, 'A new head of West Coast Finances?'

'And before I begin to make a decision I wanted to know how your fiancée would take to the idea of moving to the States. Sometimes there are family commitments…'

Alan said quickly, 'My parents died last year, so I've no family. Neither has Cass…or at least none who are close.'

Lang Dalton gave him a cool glance, and went on, 'The finance department is based at Seguro House in Los Angeles, where the two main problems are traffic and smog.

'Some people love LA, others dislike it intensely. Despite its glamorous Hollywood image, my wife hated it. That's why I transferred my administrative centre to San Francisco…

'I understand you're getting married shortly, and how a wife feels about her husband's job, and its location, can make a great deal of difference to—'

His voice thick and eager, Alan broke in, 'I'm quite sure Cass would love to live in LA. Wouldn't you, darling?'

'I would prefer Cassandra to make up her own mind,' Lang said repressively. 'The States Western Seaboard is a long way from England, and it isn't easy to leave a country one's always regarded as home.'

Then, addressing her directly, he said, 'No doubt you'll need time, a proper chance to think it over.'

In answer to Alan's appealing glance, and bearing in mind that so far nothing had been said about a job for *her*, she said carefully, 'I can tell you now that if Alan *is* offered a job in the States I would be very happy to come with him.'

His mouth wry, Lang Dalton suggested sardonically, 'Home is where the heart is?'

'Trite, but true.'

Though he gave no obvious sign, with an insight that surprised her Cassandra knew her calm answer had nettled him.

Looking at Alan, Lang said briskly, 'In that case, tomorrow morning, if you're agreeable, you'll be flown to LA. It would be advisable to spend a couple of days going through the finance department offices. That way you'll be able to see at first hand just what the post entails.

'I've asked the executive staff to be prepared to go in this weekend, so you can meet the people who, if the promotion goes through, you'll be working with. It will give you a good chance to size each other up...'

Watching their faces, Alan's open and blazing with excitement, the older man's cool and shuttered, hiding his thoughts, Cassandra felt the first prickle of apprehension.

Lang Dalton had said '*You'll* be flown to LA...*you'll* be able to see at first hand...' No mention had been made of *her* going.

But she was just being over-anxious, she assured herself firmly. He had told Alan to make her his PA, he knew they were a good team, and he had invited them *both* to California.

As though sensing her tension, Alan asked, 'What about Cass? Will she—?'

'I'm afraid any deal doesn't include a job for your future wife, though the rise in salary should more than compensate for that.'

Alan tried again. 'Only Cass is the best PA I've ever had—'

Frowning, Lang broke in, 'George Irvine already has a very experienced PA who has been with him on a part-time basis for a number of years. Miss Shulster knows all the ins and outs of our West Coast financial dealings, the kind of companies and projects we are willing to lend money to. Though she only comes in for four hours a day she should prove invaluable...'

Seeing that the younger man looked about to argue, Lang added with an air of finality, 'She has an invalid mother to care for and support, so I have no intention of disturbing the status quo. If you feel you can't fit in with the present set-up then we'll forget the whole thing.'

'Oh, no...' Alan cried hastily, 'I'm quite sure I can fit in... And Cass won't mind, I know. She's never been a *dedicated* businesswoman.'

His expression unreadable, Lang Dalton lifted his wine glass and took a sip, before saying with a touch of irony, 'Really? Yet I seem to recall from her career résumé that at university Cassandra studied market-forces and economics and graduated with a first class honours degree...?'

How in heaven's name had he remembered a thing like that? she wondered dazedly. Surely he couldn't come up with such detailed information about all his personnel?

Once again she felt disturbed, threatened.

'Or perhaps I'm mistaken?'

Looking uncomfortable, Alan began, 'No, that's quite right, and I don't mean Cass isn't excellent at her job, but she's...'

'Expendable?' Lang suggested softly.

'Certainly not... What I meant was she isn't career-minded, it isn't that important to her...'

He floundered to a stop. An only child, spoilt and pampered, he wasn't used to having to explain himself.

'You mean that you think she would be willing to sacrifice her career for yours?'

Looking a little put out at such blunt speaking, Alan admitted, 'Well, yes, but I—'

Lang glanced at her. 'Perhaps we should allow Cassandra to speak for herself?'

Irked, both by Lang Dalton's intervention and by being discussed as if she weren't present, Cassandra murmured sweetly, 'You're too kind.'

Ignoring the gleam of amusement that appeared in his dark blue eyes, she went on, 'Alan's quite right. I thoroughly enjoy my job, but I'm far from being a dedicated career woman...'

Lang regarded her, a frown drawing his well-marked brows together. He'd expected someone shrewd and calculating, hard and self-centred. This apparent willingness to put Brent's interests first had come as a surprise.

Crisply, she added, 'There are other important things in life.'

'Such as?'

'Perhaps because of my upbringing, I believe that taking care of a home and a family are of equal importance.'

There was a tense silence, before, his face curiously set and hard, Lang turned to Alan and said abruptly, 'Very well. I'll give instructions for the helicopter to be ready first thing in the morning.'

With a grateful glance at Cassandra, Alan asked, 'It will be okay for Cass to go to LA with me?'

'I think not.' Lang's answer was decisive. 'This will be business all the way, and I've never believed in mixing business and pleasure...

'Not that there would be much time for pleasure,' he added drily.

Seeing Cassandra's stricken face, Alan began, 'Oh, but couldn't she—?'

'I'm sure your fiancée can bear to part with you for just a couple of days.' Lang's tone was caustic.

As Alan looked at Cassandra helplessly, the butler returned with the final course, and a tray of coffee. Her stomach churning, Cassandra refused the chocolate and cream confection, while Alan, who had a schoolboy greed for gooey gateaux and trifles, accepted a liberal helping.

Waving away the rich sweet, Lang allowed his cup to be filled with black coffee, before turning to say to the younger man, 'All the arrangements have been made for you to spend the night at Seguro House, in the executive suite. I just need to finalize them...'

Then, with a bite, he added, 'That is, unless you've changed your mind about going? It's up to you.'

Alan finished swallowing a mouthful of chocolate and cream, and after a brief hesitation said, 'I'd prefer to leave it up to Cass.'

Cassandra drew a deep, uneven breath. Usually she was sensible and well-balanced, but there was nothing remotely sensible or well-balanced about her reaction to being left alone here with Lang Dalton.

But wasn't she exaggerating, getting worked up about nothing? They wouldn't be alone. There was a houseful of servants.

As if a houseful of servants made one iota of difference! She still dreaded the thought. And Alan must surely know how she felt?

But, in all fairness, no man in his right mind would turn down an opportunity like that. He'd done the best he could in the circumstances. Given her a chance to veto it.

A chance he knew quite well she wouldn't take.

Just for an instant she felt resentful.

Glancing up, she discovered Lang Dalton was watching her intently.

Leaning towards her, he said softly in her ear, 'You

look like Ariadne must have looked when she was about to be abandoned in Naxos.'

All at once Cassandra was convinced of two things—he was well aware of what she was thinking, and he *wanted* her to blame Alan.

Well, she wouldn't give him that satisfaction.

Allowing herself no time to change her mind, she turned to her fiancé and, with as much enthusiasm as she could muster, exclaimed, 'Darling, of course you must go!'

For a moment he looked surprised at the warm response. Then, a little lamely, he said, 'You know I don't like to leave you.'

But she'd seen the relief in his eyes.

'Don't be silly. It's only for a couple of days.'

Lang smiled grimly. A lot could happen in two days. In less time than that he'd been known to make or break a multi-million-dollar deal and, on matters that adversely affected the environment, apply enough pressure to change the *modus operandi* and ensure the results he wanted.

'Don't worry,' he told Alan urbanely. 'While you're away I'll show Cassandra something of the area, and make sure she doesn't get bored.'

If that statement of intent was meant to reassure, as far as Cassandra was concerned it failed dismally.

And Lang knew it. 'Of course if you're really not happy with that arrangement...?'

'I'm quite happy,' she assured him mendaciously.

'Well, if you change your mind before the helicopter leaves, and feel you can't bear to be abandoned after all, I might be prepared to stretch a point...' But his derisory smile suggested that it would be the behaviour of a child.

Which it would.

'Thank you, but there'll be no need.'

Lifting her chin, she met his eyes, and saw in their depths a gleam of triumph, of satisfaction.

It was almost immediately masked. But she knew without a shadow of doubt that he had got exactly what he wanted.

Remembering her premonition, she gave a shiver, suddenly convinced that, for some obscure reason, this whole thing had been carefully planned, that both she and Alan had been ruthlessly manipulated.

Such a notion had obviously never crossed Alan's mind. He tended to be inward-looking, self-absorbed, and she guessed that a lot of the byplay had gone over his head.

Off the hook, looking eager and excited once again, he turned to Lang and remarked, 'I heard through the media that you're considering putting money into the Rio Palos Dam project...'

As they drank their coffee, the two men talked business, while Cassandra tried hard to dismiss her fears. No doubt when she'd had a good night's rest she would be able to think clearly and laugh at her own foolish fancies.

Alan had slept during the interminable flight, but Cassandra, still new to flying, and perturbed about the visit, hadn't even managed to doze. Tiredness was making her skin feel as though it was drawn tight over her facial bones, and there was a dull ache between her eyes.

Making a great effort, she sat straighter and tried to concentrate on the conversation, but after a while she began to feel oddly light-headed, the male voices seemed to ebb and flow, and waves of fatigue washed over her.

'You look absolutely shattered.' Lang Dalton was on his feet by her side. 'Why don't you go to bed?'

'I think I will, if you don't mind.' To her own ears her voice sounded dazed and befuddled.

As she rose, Lang pulled out her chair and said, 'I'll see you to your room.'

'Thank you, but there's really no need,' she assured him.

Alan stood up and, a shade abstractedly, kissed her on the cheek. 'Goodnight, then, darling. I'll see you in the morning before I go.'

Leaving the two men to resume their discussion, she made her way through a house that was pleasantly cool and airy, full of evening sun and the scent of flowers.

Though she made a conscious effort to walk straight, from time to time she staggered a little, like someone who was inebriated.

As soon as she reached her room she put on her nightdress, cleaned her teeth, and, falling into bed, went to sleep the instant her head touched the pillow.

Some sound disturbed her, and she stirred and groaned. She had slept very heavily. Her head was muzzy and her throat dry.

Struggling to open eyelids that felt as though they'd been fastened shut with Velcro, she saw a strange room with bright sunshine filtering through the light muslin curtains.

For a few seconds she was utterly confused and disorientated. Then memory opened the floodgates, and along with recollection came a rush of anxiety, a return of the foreboding she'd expected sleep to banish.

Though she couldn't begin to guess at the reason, she remained convinced that, while making sure Alan went to LA, Lang Dalton had contrived that *she* should remain here... And, to all intents and purposes, of her own free will.

He was a brilliant tactician, she thought broodingly. Having put her in a position where her pride insisted she couldn't take it, he had tauntingly offered her a chance to change her mind.

Well, that had been a mistake on his part, she decided abruptly. Even if it made her look foolish, she *was* going to take it!

She would make the excuse that she had resolved to

seize this opportunity to see something of LA, in case it was going to be her future home.

Once the helicopter had dropped her, she could book herself into a hotel for the night. There would be no need for her to go anywhere near Seguro House. That way no one could accuse Alan of mixing business with pleasure.

Lang Dalton had said the helicopter would be ready 'first thing in the morning'. What time was it now? A glance at her watch only served to confuse her; she had omitted to adjust it to the time difference.

So how long had she got? At a guess she must have nearly slept the clock round, so probably not long, she thought with sudden urgency. But all she needed to do was throw a few things in her overnight bag before Alan knocked. She could always skip breakfast.

Jumping out of bed, she hurried to the bathroom.

Having showered and dressed at top speed, and pulled a brush through her long hair, she began to pack some changes of clothing and a few essentials. She had barely finished when she heard the unmistakable sound of a helicopter.

Just in the nick of time, she thought with relief. Any second now Alan would be knocking at the door.

But no knock came, and it took a moment or two of stunned disbelief before the unwelcome fact finally sank in that the engine noise, rather than approaching, was moving *away*.

No, no, it *couldn't* be. Alan wouldn't leave without seeing her, without saying goodbye.

Her heart suddenly racing, she pressed a button set into the side of the nearest arch, and the glass panels slid aside.

Hurrying out onto the patio, she shielded her eyes from the brightness and looked up into the cloudless sky. The helicopter, silver against the deep blue, was heading south-west towards the coast and the urban sprawl that was Los Angeles...

'Good morning.' Lang Dalton's low-pitched, attractive voice made her jump. 'You're up and dressed earlier than I'd expected.'

Bare feet leaving wet prints, he was coming towards her, tanned and fit-looking, wearing well-cut navy swimming trunks, a towel slung around his neck. His thick blond hair was wet and rumpled, a single lock falling over his forehead.

'That isn't...?' Her voice shook betrayingly, and she stopped speaking abruptly.

Following her gaze to where the helicopter had become a rapidly dwindling speck, he said, 'I'm afraid so,' adding with a kind of mocking concern, 'You look upset. I do hope you hadn't changed your mind about going?'

'No, I hadn't changed my mind,' she lied jerkily, and felt almost sure that he didn't believe her. 'But Alan promised he'd...' Once again she was forced to stop.

'See you before he left?' Lang finished for her. 'You'll have to forgive him. He didn't have a moment to spare. In fact he was forced to go without any breakfast.'

A drop of water ran down his lean cheek and he lifted the towel to wipe it away before continuing, 'The helicopter arrived over an hour early. Some last-minute problem had cropped up that meant McDowell, my pilot, was needed back in LA urgently.'

But surely Alan could have found just a few seconds to say goodbye?

As though reading her thoughts, Lang went on smoothly, 'Brent and I agreed that as you were obviously jet-lagged it would be a shame to wake you for what would have necessarily been a very brief farewell.'

Brent and I agreed... Cassandra bit her lip vexedly. Reading between the lines, what it amounted to was that to make sure she didn't change her mind and take advantage of his offer Lang Dalton had tried to prevent Alan from waking her.

And Alan, no doubt feeling uncomfortable about leaving her, and possibly fearing some kind of last-minute reproach, had taken the easy way out.

Aloud, she said, 'How thoughtful of you both.' And, feeling caught, *trapped*, wondered despairingly how she was going to get through the next two days.

But somehow she would have to, and with the best possible grace...

As though applauding her unspoken decision, Lang smiled at her, and said briskly, 'However, as you *are* awake, you've time for a swim before breakfast.'

The blue, sparkling water looked very inviting, but she found herself oddly unwilling to appear in front of him in a swimsuit.

'I'm not sure what the time is,' she prevaricated. 'I forgot to alter my watch.'

Glancing at the slim, waterproof Rolex he wore on his left wrist, Lang told her, 'It's just after six.' Then, with a glint, he said, 'And I can recommend that swim.'

Making a big deal of adjusting her watch, she half shook her head. 'I'm really thirsty. I think I'd rather have a drink.'

'Why not have both? There's some freshly squeezed juice waiting.' He indicated a table by the pool-side that had been set with a selection of fruit and cereals, a jug of orange juice and two tall glasses.

As she hesitated, his sardonic smile making it clear that he had recognized the reason for her reluctance, he added, 'I'm going in now to shower and dress. Afterwards I've got a couple of things to take care of, so you've a good half-hour before I join you for breakfast.'

'Thank you; in that case I think I will.' She was pleased that her voice was steady.

Watching him walk away, his carriage easy, athletic, she gritted her teeth. He was the most complex, demoralizing, *disturbing* man she'd ever met.

Going back into her room, the first thing she noticed was the overnight bag that now wouldn't be needed.

Oh, if only she'd wakened sooner! Agitated and jumpy, nervous as a cat shut in the wrong house, she sighed. But it was too late. There was nothing she could do but make the best of things.

Stripping off her clothes, she pulled on her black swimsuit and looked in the cheval-glass. It fitted her slender, long-legged figure to perfection, and by modern standards was quite modest, but her heightened sensibilities made her feel half naked.

A cautious peep showed the patio was deserted, and, with a rueful grimace at the stupidity of her own behaviour, she ventured out.

She helped herself to a glass of the delicious, sweet-tart juice, and drank it thirstily before slipping into the pool.

The water was blissfully cool and refreshing, and she swam several leisurely lengths while the tension slowly drained out of her.

Turning on her back, she floated motionless, her hair fanning out around her, her eyes closed, the Californian sun warm on her face.

'About ready?'

Lang's voice startled her, and her head went under. She gulped in water, and for a second or two thrashed about wildly.

A strong hand caught one of her wrists and drew her to the side. Then, crouching, he took her under her arms and hauled her out with what seemed to be effortless ease.

While she coughed and spluttered, he set her on her feet and steadied her until she'd blinked the water from her eyes and got her breath back. Then, picking up a short white towelling robe he'd tossed over a chair, he held it for her.

'Thank you,' she said huskily. Pulling the robe around

her, she knotted the belt and used the cowl collar to wipe her face and dry the dripping ends of her hair.

A hint of amusement in his voice, Lang suggested, 'Perhaps in future you should avoid the deep end, rather than risk drowning.'

'I can swim perfectly well,' she informed him indignantly. 'I would have been in no danger of drowning if you hadn't startled me.'

She hadn't meant to sound quite so *accusing*, she thought belatedly, but the shock had momentarily put out of her head the need to tread warily.

'I'm sorry. Trying to drown you wasn't my intention. Believe me, I much prefer you alive.' Then he said softly, 'You see, I have plans for you, Cassandra.'

'Plans?' A little chill of alarm ran down her spine. 'What kind of plans?'

'You'll have to wait and see. I've always believed that anticipation hones the…' There was a brief pause before he added, 'Pleasure. Now, are you ready for some breakfast?'

He had changed into lightweight trousers and a blue open-necked sports shirt. Conscious that he was studying the slim length of her bare legs, and feeling very much at a disadvantage, she stammered, 'I—I was hoping to get dressed first.'

A hand beneath her elbow, he urged her towards the table and the appetizing smell of coffee. 'This is California. Even up here, where the air's cooler, you're already wearing more than you need.'

Seeing nothing else for it, she sat down, hiding her legs under the table.

Smiling a little, he took his own seat and poured coffee for them both, before asking, 'Would you like to start with some cereal?' When she shook her head, he helped her to scrambled eggs and thin slices of crispy bacon.

Sitting in the sun, a balmy breeze rustling the palm fronds and wafting the scent of frangipani, the mountains making a majestic backdrop, they ate in silence, Lang looking relaxed and easy, Cassandra anything but.

What had he meant by *plans?* she wondered uneasily. It had sounded almost like a veiled threat...

Oh, don't be a fool! she scolded herself crossly. What possible reason could a man in his position have for threatening her? Until the previous day she'd never even met him, let alone given him any cause to want to harm her.

Lang Dalton was her boss, nothing more or less. A wealthy, influential, highly respected entrepreneur, not some kind of bogeyman.

Probably *plans* had been a reference to some quite innocuous outing. He'd told Alan that he would show her 'something of the area'.

When, eating abstractedly, she'd done justice to the meal, Lang refilled her cup and, his voice casual, said, 'Oh, by the way, your fiancé wrote you a note while he was snatching a quick coffee.'

Why hadn't he mentioned it before? she wondered vexedly.

As though in answer to that thought, he added with an ironic smile, 'In the general excitement, I'm afraid it almost slipped my mind.'

Feeling in the pocket of his shirt, he produced a folded piece of paper and handed it to her.

Confirming Alan's haste, his almost painfully neat writing had degenerated into a scrawl.

Cass, darling, sorry to leave without seeing you, but in the circumstances it seemed a shame to disturb you. While we were talking last night, Mr Dalton told me where he planned to take you, so enjoy your weekend, and I'll catch up with you in Las Vegas Sunday evening.
Love, A.

Looking up, Cassandra asked blankly, 'Las Vegas?'

'I thought you might like to see the place,' Lang said easily. 'We can drive over to Nevada—you'll find the journey itself is a pleasure—and stay a couple of nights at the Golden Phoenix... I've arranged for your fiancé to be flown straight there from LA...

'Apart from the fact that Vegas is well worth seeing for its own sake—it was a frontier outpost and railway town before becoming a gambling mecca—it's surrounded by some magnificent desert scenery.

'Death Valley lies to the west, and from nearby McCarran International Airport there are flights that offer a bird's-eye view of the Grand Canyon.'

'That sounds wonderful,' she admitted, feeling both excited and relieved. A trip to Las Vegas in a chauffeur-driven car, and staying at a hotel with plenty of people, had to be a great deal easier than remaining here with only Lang Dalton for company.

'I'm glad you approve.' *So far so good,* he thought, and asked softly, 'Are you anything of a gambler, Cassandra?'

'No. Are you?'

He smiled thinly. 'Not in the usual sense. I have been known to play for high stakes, but only when the odds are stacked in my favour.'

Something about his answer made her feel uneasy, but, telling herself that she mustn't start imagining things again, she asked, 'When do you plan to start?'

'As soon as possible. How long will it take you to get ready?'

'Ten minutes?'

Nodding his approval, he rose to his feet and pulled out her chair.

CHAPTER THREE

As quickly as she could, Cassandra showered, put on a white, slim-fitting shift dress, and wound her hair into a neat coil. Her overnight bag in her hand, she was descending the terrace steps when a big cream and beige four-wheel drive appeared with Lang at the wheel.

Her heart sank a little. It seemed he intended to drive himself.

Jumping out, he tossed her luggage on to the back seat alongside his own and, a hand beneath her bare elbow, helped her into the air-conditioned vehicle.

'Ten minutes exactly,' he congratulated her, adding, his smile crooked, 'With having your overnight things to pack, I hardly thought you'd make it in time...'

So he *hadn't* believed her when she'd denied changing her mind, and he knew quite well that her bag had been already packed.

Damn him! she thought crossly, flustered by both his touch and his ironic words.

'And you even manage to look cool and collected, and incredibly beautiful.'

Pursing her lips, she said, 'Thank you, Mr Dalton.'

Laughing at her primness, he urged, 'Have a heart, Cassandra... For the weekend at least, forget I'm your boss and call me Lang.'

Not on your life! she decided grimly. Calling him by his first name would add a new dimension, a complication she would rather not tangle with.

A moment later he was in the driving seat, and with a throaty roar from the powerful engine they were off, following a private road through extensive, palm-shaded grounds.

He drove without speaking, his lean, long-fingered hands lying lightly on the wheel, a slight smile touching his firm mouth.

The tall, wrought-iron gates in the perimeter wall slid aside at their approach and closed behind them as they turned to follow a tortuous mountain road between spectacular masses of granite boulders and tinder-dry scrub.

But rather than watching the scenery Cassandra's eyes were irresistibly drawn to her companion's hard-boned profile—the strong nose, the controlled line of the upper lip in direct contrast to the warm curve of the lower, the droop of an eyelid at the outer corner, the sweep of thick, gold-tipped lashes...

As though aware of her scrutiny, he suddenly turned his head to smile at her. Feeling herself start to flush, she looked hurriedly away.

For a while she stared determinedly out of the window, absently noting a gnarled, twisted cypress and the occasional sword-leaved yucca.

Then, wanting to break the silence, to get on some kind of workable footing that would keep a respectable distance between them, she asked politely, 'Do you go to Las Vegas often?'

'From time to time,' he answered casually.

Remembering his previous remarks, she suggested, 'But not to gamble?'

He shook his head. 'Sometimes it's a matter of business. Other times I go to catch one of the big name acts when they appear at Caesar's Palace or the Golden Phoenix.'

'Earlier you spoke as if you enjoyed the journey?'

'I do. I've always got a buzz from just being on the move. Unfortunately my wife didn't. Nina found any kind of travelling both tiring and boring...

'Do you enjoy being on the move, Cassandra?'

'Yes, I do.' Her voice wistful, she added, 'I'd like to have done some real travelling, seen a lot more of the world.'

But she'd had neither the opportunity nor the money. Having sent her to a good school, her parents had considered their duty done, and, unwilling to ask them for anything further, she'd struggled to be completely independent.

Lang slanted her a glance. 'You said you'd been to Paris?'

'Yes.'

'When was that?'

Unwilling to talk about it, she answered shortly, 'A couple of months ago.'

'With Brent?'

Lifting her chin, she said, 'Yes.'

'Did you enjoy it?'

'Yes.'

In fact the weekend had proved to be something of a disaster and they'd ended up sleeping in separate beds. Yet in an odd sort of way the truth coming out had strengthened their relationship, and resulted in their deciding to get married earlier than first planned.

Afraid Lang was going to question her further, she abruptly changed the subject, saying the first thing that came into her head. 'As today's journey seems to be a longish one, I'd half expected you to take the limousine.'

He went along with it. 'On this kind of trip I prefer to drive myself, and the Cherokee was bought primarily for desert travel, which needs special safety precautions.'

'You make it sound...dangerous.'

'In spite of its beauty, it can be just that. Particularly in the hottest months when the temperature in Death Valley has been known to reach a hundred and thirty-four degrees Fahrenheit. Anyone who breaks down or gets stuck in such desiccating heat can be in real trouble, unless they have plenty of water and some way of shielding themselves from the sun until help arrives.'

'Which I'm sure we have?' she asked gravely.

With a sidelong glance, he answered equally gravely, 'Of course.'

Only the sudden gleam in his blue eyes told her he knew he was being teased.

It was a new, and unexpected, experience for him. Still, a lot about this woman had been unexpected, he admitted. Her spirit and her sense of humour, her innocence...

Innocence?

No! He *knew* that appearance of innocence was assumed. There had been Sean... And she and Brent were undoubtedly lovers. But what really had come as a surprise was that she seemed to genuinely love the man whose ring she was wearing.

In the circumstances, an unlooked-for complication.

Until he'd met her, he'd presumed she would be out for all she could get, willing to ditch Brent when some more lucrative proposition offered itself.

Now he had serious doubts. He might be forced to use his alternative plan. But what did it matter so long as, in the end, he got what he wanted...?

'Are we actually going through Death Valley?' Her low, slightly husky voice broke into his thoughts.

'I thought you might like to see it. But if you don't care for the idea...?'

'Oh, I do!' There was no mistaking her eagerness. 'I'm really looking forward to it...'

And she wasn't disappointed. The scenery was everything Lang had said it would be, and, setting aside all her previous doubts and fears, she enjoyed every moment of the dramatic and varied terrain.

Driving through the valley, with its well-tarmacked road running between wide stretches of sandy scrub and flanked by the distant and spectacular mountain ranges, proved to be breathtaking.

They reached Furnace Creek at midday and stopped for what turned out to be an excellent meal, before resuming their journey.

Since he'd suggested that she use his first name, there had been a complete change in his attitude. Any suggestion of boss and employee had gone and he was treating her simply as a pleasant companion.

Some of her earlier wariness had vanished, put to flight by his casual friendliness. She thought, almost with a sense of wonder, that it might have been relatively easy to relax and enjoy his company, if she hadn't been so aware of, and so bothered by, his powerful masculinity.

While they clocked up the miles and the afternoon wore on, in answer to her interested questions, Lang told her about some of his earlier travels.

As a young man he'd visited most of the States, it appeared, but, having a liking for desert county, Nevada, Arizona and New Mexico had remained amongst his favourites.

Dusk had begun to fall before they stopped for a quick bite at Minnie's Diner, a roadside café more notable for its truckers-sized portions than any attempt at elegance.

Cassandra was surprised that a man like Lang Dalton would choose to eat at what was in effect a transport café.

He picked it up immediately. 'Perhaps, like Nina, you'd prefer to stop somewhere more up-market?'

'No, it's all part of the fun,' she assured him cheerfully, taking a seat at a plastic-topped table. 'And if it's anything like England the food in this kind of place is usually good, as well as cheap.'

'When did you discover that?'

'While I was a student. My room-mate and I, and one or two others in our year, had an occasional meal at Joe's. A plate of shepherds's pie made a change from baked beans on toast, and helped to keep body and soul together.'

'You were short of money?'

'Perpetually,' she said drily.

'Didn't your parents help?'

'No. I didn't ask them to.'

An expression in his dark blue eyes she was unable to read, his voice deceptively casual, he remarked, 'With your kind of beauty it should have been easy to find yourself a well-off boyfriend.'

The words were like a kick in the solar plexus.

All the colour draining from her face, her stomach tying itself in a knot of remembered fear and pain, she fought for breath.

Noting her sudden pallor, made more pronounced by the harsh glare of the overhead lights, he queried solicitously, 'Something wrong?'

She shook her head. 'No.'

'You look very pale.'

'I'm fine.' Avoiding his eyes, she studied a finger-marked menu propped against a ketchup bottle. 'What do you suggest?'

He answered levelly, 'It depends how hungry you are.'

'Not very.' Her appetite had just deserted her.

'Then perhaps a bagel with ham or cheese or, if you want something a shade more exciting, a BLT on your choice of bread.'

A tired-looking, middle-aged waitress wearing a pink nylon overall and down-at-heel mules was already hovering, her eyes fixed on Lang. 'The pastrami's good,' she offered.

He nodded. 'Then make mine pastrami on rye.'

Pulling herself together, determinedly pushing away the traumas of the past, Cassandra decided, 'I think I will plump for a little excitement. I'll try a BLT on sour-dough.'

When the waitress had flip-flopped away, Lang asked, a gleam in his eye, 'Does your decision to "plump for a little excitement" extend to other things?'

Instantly wary, she said stiffly, 'That depends on what you mean by *other things.*'

He smiled, mocking her caution. 'A mild flutter in the casino, for instance?'

'I don't think I'm cut out to be a gambler,' she told him.

'Well, you can't visit a place like Vegas without giving it a whirl. If you don't fancy the big-time stuff there are slot machines everywhere. Casinos have them, Laundromats have them, even instant wedding chapels have them...'

He talked idly about Las Vegas until their food arrived: a pile of thinly sliced smoked beef on rye bread, and a bacon, lettuce and tomato sandwich she had to use both hands to pick up.

By the time they'd eaten, and drunk good strong coffee from thick mugs, darkness was pressing against the steamy windows.

'We'd better get going,' Lang observed, and, leaving an extremely liberal tip, escorted her out to the waiting car.

For Cassandra, the rest of the drive captured the essence of all the road movies she'd ever seen. With no scenery to look at, Lang stepped on the gas, and, insects splattering against the windscreen, they drove through the hot night like a tornado.

As they stormed east, the highway wound on, black and practically deserted, and Cassandra began to appreciate the vastness of the country they were travelling through.

Eventually she must have dozed, because she surfaced to find Lang touching her shoulder. 'Wake up,' he said softly. 'You mustn't miss this.'

'Miss what?' She stifled a yawn.

'Your first sight of Las Vegas.'

From their elevated position, she could see that below, and ahead of them, rising from the black desert floor like some night-time mirage, was a colourful, shimmering, many-faceted pool of light. Its glow set the sky on fire.

'That's magical,' she breathed.

'This particular sight never fails to move me,' he admitted.

She agreed. 'I can see why.' And thought what an enigma this man was. Beneath his surface hardness, he had depth and sensitivity, a real feeling for beauty.

They drove into town and along the Strip. On every side, neon signs flashed—diamond horseshoes, silver garters, gold nuggets, pink champagne pouring endlessly into slippers, multi-coloured cascades of stardust—a deluge of brilliant and garish light, as each place tried to out-dazzle the competition.

Then, jammed between the Red Rooster pizza-parlour and a wildly futuristic hotel, bizarre and totally incongruous, was an instant wedding chapel. Its white, neon cross was surrounded by glowing artificial lilies and flashing lights.

Through its open door could be glimpsed a couple, the man in a rhinestone jacket, the woman wearing a red dress covered in glittering sequins and flowers in her hair, waiting on a bench.

Leaving the theatrical flamboyance of the Strip behind them, they came at last to the Golden Phoenix, a huge, handsome, white-marble building, with a colonnaded portico.

Standing well back from the street, its wide, paved forecourt allowing access to an underground car park, it looked to be quiet and select, in a class of its own.

'Is it simply a hotel?' Cassandra queried as they drew up in front of the steps.

Lang jumped out and came round to help her out. 'It's a hotel and casino combined.'

Looking up at the golden phoenix that graced the entrance, she remarked, 'I like the name.'

He grinned. 'The people who come here regularly just refer to it as Dalton's.'

'So you own it?'

Escorting her inside, Lang replied drily, 'Dalton Enterprises does.'

Which amounted to the same thing.

The foyer was palatial, with a huge marble fountain, hanging gardens and crystal chandeliers.

'Evening, Stephens...' Lang tossed the car keys to a dapper, middle-aged man behind the reception desk and, a hand at Cassandra's waist, led her towards a private elevator. 'Will you see that our luggage is taken up to my suite immediately, and the car put away?'

'Certainly, Mr Dalton.'

As the doors slid to behind them, her voice betraying her sudden agitation, she blurted out, 'You're expecting me to share your suite?'

His face perfectly straight, he queried, 'Does that worry you?'

Something in his manner convinced her he was teasing. Determined not to fall for it, she asked with what coolness she could muster, 'Should it?'

'Only if you sleepwalk,' he answered succinctly.

As she might have expected his marble-floored penthouse suite was both elegant and spacious, with Kashmir rugs and long windows curtained in fine muslin and heavy, gold velvet drapes.

From the foyer, a door led into an attractively furnished central sitting-room with a striking pale blue and gold decor. On either side there was a luxurious, ivory-carpeted bedroom and *en-suite* bathroom, one in delicate shades of pink and oyster, the other decorated in straw and off-white.

Lang indicated the latter. 'That's the room I usually

use, but feel free to choose.' His smile was openly mocking. 'I believe both doors lock.'

'Thank you,' she said stiffly, 'I'll be quite happy with the other one.'

As she finished speaking, a bellboy appeared with their small amount of luggage, and left clutching a generous tip.

Picking up her bag, she said, 'I'd like to take a quick shower and change, if that's all right?'

'Of course. Say fifteen minutes?'

Though she was a couple of minutes early, Lang was waiting for her in the sitting-room, his thick blond hair smoothly brushed, his jaw freshly shaven.

He looked both suave and handsome, the hard-edged, potentially ruthless element overlaid with a veneer of polished sophistication.

After one glance at his immaculate evening clothes, Cassandra knew herself to be underdressed. 'I'm afraid this is all I have with me,' she explained apologetically.

His unsparing glance took in the simple black cocktail dress, the silk-clad legs and high-heeled sandals, the complete lack of jewellery.

Flatly, he said, 'As far as I'm concerned you look fine, but if it bothers you there are plenty of excellent boutiques in the shopping mall...'

As she half shook her head, he suggested, 'Then shall we go down?'

A minute later they were back in the sumptuous main foyer. Opening a door on the left, marked 'Private', Lang ushered Cassandra into a large and well-furnished sitting-room.

Obviously they'd been expected. On a low table was an oval silver tray with three glasses and a bottle of vintage champagne in an ice bucket.

A fair-haired man of medium height, wearing evening clothes, rose from an armchair which faced an array of monitors. He was in his early thirties, about the same age as Lang, she judged, thin-faced and pleasant-looking, with a wide, friendly smile.

'Lang, great to see you!'

When the two men, obviously old friends, had shaken hands, Lang put an arm around Cassandra's waist and said, 'Honey, I'd like you to meet Robert Laski. He manages the Golden Phoenix for me... Rob, this is Cassandra Vallance.'

Disconcerted by the possessive arm and the 'honey', she stammered, 'H-how do you do?'

Taking her hand, Rob said warmly, 'It's very nice to meet you. I hope you won't mind if I call you Cassandra?'

'No, not at all.'

'Won't you sit down?'

Trying to regain her composure, she took a seat on a comfortable settee, while Rob moved to open the champagne.

'How are things going?' Lang queried, remaining standing.

'Fine,' Rob answered, 'apart from one slight problem...' Pausing to fill three champagne flutes, he handed one to Cassandra—his glance resting for an instant on the glittering diamond cluster on her engagement finger—and another to Lang, before raising his own glass in a silent toast.

When they had all drunk a little of the sparkling wine, he continued, 'Earlier tonight a Mr Hoke Donelly—not one of our regular clientele—booked in, saying he'd like a flutter.

'He was quiet and well-dressed, so they let him go through to the casino. His game was poker, and for a while he was on a winning streak. Then his luck turned and he started to lose steadily. Instead of stopping, he began to plunge more heavily...'

Lang sighed. 'The old, old story.'

'He'd lost almost five thousand dollars before his chips ran out... When he asked to play on credit they sent him to me.

'Donelly's young and green and should never have been gambling at all. When I questioned him he admitted he'd been using money he and his fiancée had saved to get married. It seems the girl's pregnant, and tonight was a desperate one-off bid to get rich quickly.

'They were negotiating a loan to buy a house of their own, rather than have to live with her parents, who strongly disapprove of the match, but a few days ago he lost his job...'

Sipping her champagne, Cassandra could only feel heartily sorry for the hapless pair.

'He confessed that coming to Vegas was his idea, and the girl had been reluctant. That's why he was so anxious to keep on playing until he'd at least recouped his losses.'

With a grimace, Rob added, 'As things stand, the young idiot hasn't enough left to even pay for his room, let alone get back to Denver.'

'Where is he now?' Lang sounded angry.

'I asked him to wait in the office until you got here. I take it you won't allow him credit?'

'Certainly not. He'll only dig himself in deeper...'

While forced to agree that Lang was probably right, Cassandra felt cold, chilled by his ruthlessness.

'Give him a room for the night and his money back, and tell him, in future, not to be such a damn fool.'

When Rob had disappeared to do his bidding, Cassandra said with undisguised relief, 'That was extremely generous of you. I thought at first you were angry.'

'I *am* angry.' He refilled her glass, and added, 'They should never have allowed him to play in the first place. It's just the sort of thing I try to guard against.

'The only clientele I want are the rich and experienced

who play for kicks, and who, if they lose, can well afford it. Donelly's kind of gambling is a mug's game, as he's no doubt realized. His luck was out and—'

'Personally I think his luck was *in*,' Cassandra stated firmly.

'What makes you say that?'

'If he'd lost his money in any other casino, I can't believe they would have been so…charitable.'

Lang shook his head. 'Don't put me down as soft, or altruistic. I just don't want that kind of thing on my conscience.'

'It wouldn't worry a lot of people.'

Curtly he said, 'Perhaps my conscience already carries a big enough burden.'

As she was wondering what he meant by that, the door opened and Rob came back. 'I rather think Donelly's learnt his lesson. He was almost abjectly grateful, and if you've got a minute he'd like to thank you in person.'

'You have his home address?'

'It's in the register.'

Lang turned to Cassandra. 'If you'll excuse me for a while? Rob will show you round the casino and provide you with some chips so you can try your hand at the tables.'

Steadily she said, 'I'd love to have a look round, but I really can't afford to gamble.'

'A few hundred dollars on the house won't break the bank,' Lang assured her cheerfully. Taking her hand, he smiled down at her. 'I'll rejoin you shortly.'

Before she could even guess his intention he used the hand he was holding to draw her to him. Bending his head, he touched his lips to hers, rocking her world, leaving her flustered and breathless, her pulses racing.

He had kissed her as though he had a right, and, taken by surprise, she made no protest. When Rob turned towards the door, she followed him on legs that felt like warm jelly.

As he escorted her across the foyer, needing to find something to say, to regain her equilibrium, she harked back to the young gambler. 'Does that kind of thing happen often?'

'You mean Donelly? No, not often. And when it does Lang invariably steps in. Though he's no soft touch, he cares about people.

'He has interests in Denver, and when he's checked that Donelly's story is true it's quite on the cards that he'll not only give him a job but loan him the money to buy a house…'

Cassandra sighed. Lang Dalton was a complete mystery. Though she no longer believed he was hard and ruthless, she was miles from understanding either him or his motives.

Why on earth had he kissed her? Was he planning to try and seduce her?

No, surely not. For one thing he was still mourning his wife. For another, why try to seduce one of his own staff, and another man's fiancée? If he wanted a woman, in a place like Las Vegas he would have no difficulty finding one.

Or any other place for that matter, given his looks and charisma. Not to mention his money.

But if he *was* hoping to take *her* to bed, despite his magnetism, which in a strange kind of way she couldn't help but respond to, she would have no difficulty in keeping him at bay.

Apart from the fact that she would never let Alan down, she knew herself protected by the remembered fear and trauma that even the man she loved had so far been unable to overcome…

'Here we are.' Rob's voice broke into her thoughts. 'This is where the rich and famous come to get their kicks…' He opened a door and ushered her into a huge circular room.

The air-conditioned casino was windowless, lit by

golden phoenix wall-lamps and crystal chandeliers. Its ivory and gold decor was both elegant and luxurious. There were several rooms leading off, where, Rob told her, private games of poker and such like were held.

'And that's the stage for the big-name entertainers.' He indicated a raised dais in the centre where, seated at a white baby grand, a woman in a clinging silver dress was quietly playing and singing the blues.

From that axis, gaming tables manned by croupiers fanned out like the spokes of a wheel. The staff were impeccably dressed, the men in evening jackets, the women in glamorous black gowns. All wore a discreet, but unmistakable, gold phoenix, either in the form of a pin or a brooch.

What seemed like a small army of waitresses were moving about with trays of champagne and caviare, smoked salmon sandwiches and cocktails.

Apart from the singer, the well-modulated voices of the croupiers, the rattle of dice and the click of roulette wheels, there was very little noise, and to Cassandra's surprise the atmosphere was calm, almost laid-back, more like a select club than a casino.

She had expected a din, razzle-dazzle, electric tension, and lots of excitement.

When she said as much, Rob laughed. 'This is the up-market version of a gambling joint. You can get all that glittering razzmatazz, or at least a tinsel version of it, on the Strip.

'The casinos there are quite different. Most of them are lined with batteries of fruit machines, known as Super-Loose Slots, that ''slot professionals'' stand at and feed with silver dollars...

'Oh, and speaking of dollars...' He felt in his pocket and produced a handful of thin golden discs each stamped with a phoenix and what looked like a short code. 'Here's some plastic money to be going on with. What would you like to try your hand at?'

'Roulette, I think,' she said doubtfully.

He led her to a table with two free seats and sat down by her side, stacking the chips into neat piles. The croupier welcomed them with a smile, and an instant later a waitress was serving them champagne.

Glancing round the table, Cassandra saw that the colour of the chips varied, and asked why.

'It depends on their value,' Rob explained. 'They start from fifty dollars…'

While the wheel spun and the ball rattled from slot to slot, he told her the rudiments of the game. 'You pick a number and a colour, either red or black, then put as many chips as you want to bet on that particular square…'

Unwilling to chance losing money that wasn't her own, she placed two chips on black 7, and watched the wheel spin until it finally slowed and the ball clicked into red 3.

A moment later the croupier's rake was whisking her stake away, and the whole thing started over again.

Cassandra quickly found that, as she'd suspected, she was no gambler. Several other people playing seemed to find the game enthralling, but to her it soon became boring and repetitive.

When the waitress brought more champagne, already starting to feel slightly muzzy, she shook her head and, thirsty, accepted a glass of fruit juice decorated with cherries and mint leaves.

It was cool and refreshing and easy to drink. The second it was gone, another appeared at her elbow as if by magic.

She had swallowed more than half of it before she overheard the elegantly dressed woman sitting next to her, who was drinking the same, refer to it as a vodka cocktail.

By casino standards the night had hardly begun, but

she was tired, still suffering from the effects of jet lag, and before long it became even harder to concentrate.

A man came up and spoke quietly to Rob who, after a moment, turned to Cassandra and said, 'I hope you don't mind if I leave you? Lang should be here any minute.'

'No, of course I don't mind.'

'Would you like any more chips?'

Shaking her head, she said, 'No, thank you.' She had already lost count of the amount she'd lost. It must be several hundred dollars.

Stifling a yawn, she sat up straighter, but she found it difficult to focus. The rattles and clicks were soporific, and the spinning wheel had become a hypnotic blur. When Lang came she would excuse herself and tell him...

Before the thought was completed, he had slipped into the empty chair by her side. 'Having fun?'

Turning to look into his hard-boned face, she answered politely, 'Yes, thank you.' Then, handing him her few remaining chips, she added, 'But I'm rather tired. I'd like to go to bed.'

'I'll see you up.'

'Really, there's no need,' she protested. 'Please don't leave on my account.'

'It isn't on your account.' A hand beneath her elbow, he helped her to her feet. 'I don't want to be too late myself.'

As she reluctantly accompanied him to the elevator, all her earlier doubts and fears that he might be hoping to seduce her suddenly returned.

Biting back her alarm, she reminded herself that if he did try anything, though it would undoubtedly prove embarrassing to have to freeze him off, she was in no danger.

CHAPTER FOUR

THEY reached the suite to find a trolley was waiting with a selection of delicious-looking open sandwiches, a pot of coffee keeping hot, and a bottle of Krug on ice.

When Cassandra would have said a hasty goodnight and headed for her room, Lang suggested, 'I thought we might have a glass of champagne first...'

'Not for me, thank you.' She was still feeling light-headed and slightly muzzy. 'I've had more than enough to drink for one night.'

'Then what about a sandwich...?'

His face was guileless, his approach relaxed, friendly, with no hint of pressure. Finding nothing in either his looks or his manner to alarm her, she decided a little sheepishly that she had misjudged him.

'You could probably use some food.'

After three glasses of champagne and two cocktails, something to eat might not be a bad idea.

She nodded, and, having helped herself to a selection of the dainty sandwiches, went to sit in one of the low armchairs.

Lang brought his own plate and took a seat opposite. His voice casual, he queried, 'What did you think of Rob?'

'I liked him very much,' she said sincerely. Adding, 'I got the impression that you know each other very well?'

'Rob was the first friend I made when I came to the States. His parents owned the house next door.'

'So you weren't born over here?' She found herself wanting to know more about him.

'No. I lived in England until I was nine. My mother was a Londoner and my father a Californian with Anglo-American business interests. Their marriage was a mistake from the word go, and when it finally broke up my mother stayed in England and I went to the States with my father.'

It was a flat, dispassionate statement of facts, but Cassandra was oddly convinced that he'd been badly affected by the break-up.

'Was that your own choice?'

'No. It was my father's price for agreeing to a speedy, uncontested divorce.'

'Were you an only child?'

'No, I had a younger sister whom I adored. Katy, who was just five, stayed with our mother.'

'You must have missed them.'

It was a comment rather than a question, but he answered briefly, 'I did.'

Then, with the first trace of a barely hidden bitterness, he said, 'But I wasn't allowed to show it. It would have been a sign of weakness, and my father wouldn't tolerate any sign of weakness. He was a strict disciplinarian who equated having feelings with being soft.'

'Did you keep in touch with your mother?' Cassandra asked quietly.

'I wanted to, but my father wouldn't allow it. He pointed out that she couldn't have loved me, otherwise she wouldn't have let me go. And after a while I realized he was right. She must have known what a cold, harsh man my father was, what my life would be like. She could have just left him and kept both my sister and myself. But she wanted a divorce so she could marry her long-term lover, and I was expendable.' Now the bitterness was open and searing.

Knowing only too well what it was like to feel unloved and unwanted, Cassandra felt a deep pity for the unhappy child he must have been.

Swallowing hard, she asked, 'Didn't your father want both his children?'

'No. Just a son to follow in his footsteps. And in any case we *weren't* both his children. Katy was my half-sister, my mother's lover's daughter, and the one who mattered to her.

'But I never held that against Katy—' for the first time Lang's face softened '—and I never stopped missing her. When I knew she would be old enough to understand, with Rob's help, I began to write to her in secret. More often than not Rob gave me the money for the postage, and I used to put his address on the letters.

'Eventually she started to write back. She said she could still remember me; she said she still loved me and missed me. Whenever she wrote, she asked if I could go and see her.'

'Did you manage to?'

Lang shook his head. 'There were times when I was tempted to tell my father the truth and ask him for the air fare, but I knew it would be no use.

'Though his business was finance and he was a wealthy man, he didn't believe in ''making his son soft''. He'd always forced me to fight for everything I wanted, and grovel for every cent he gave me.'

Cassandra bit her lip, feeling a fierce anger against a man who would treat his own son that way.

His face dark and brooding, Lang continued bleakly, 'I didn't find grovelling easy. I preferred to mow lawns, wash cars, run errands, sweep leaves…whatever…

'The minute I was able, I left home, and, taking evening and weekend jobs, worked my way through college…'

So he knew as well as she did what it was like to be a struggling student.

'I'd just finished sitting my final exams when my father dropped dead with a heart attack…I didn't feel a thing. No sadness. No regret. He would have been pleased with me.

'As soon as I could raise the fare I went over to England. Katy, the only person in the world who had ever cared a damn, was delighted to see me. My mother *said* she was, but it was obvious she felt guilty and ill at ease. Her second husband had run off with another woman, so there was only the two of them. They were having a hard time, struggling to manage. My mother was suffering from a debilitating disease, and Katy, who was a brilliant cellist, had just started at the Royal College of Music.

'I used my father's money to help them.' Flatly, he added, 'My mother died not long afterwards.'

'Do you still see your sister?'

His face tightened into a white mask of pain and anger. With difficulty, as though the words hurt, he said, 'She and her husband were killed in a car crash some eighteen months ago.'

It was plain that his sister's tragic death had left a wound that had remained unhealed. And on top of that he had lost a wife he must have loved dearly.

Cassandra's heart bled for him. A feeling of compassion, a tenderness that was almost maternal, made her want to reach out and touch him, to tell him how sorry she was.

Before she could do either, his face wiped clear of all emotion, he said abruptly, 'I'm sorry. You'll have to forgive me. You're too good a listener. But believe me, I hadn't intended to bore you like this...'

'I'm not bored,' she assured him, 'and I'm glad you've told me.'

'You're the only person, apart from Rob, who knows the sorry tale.'

Yes, she could believe he didn't bare his feelings often.

Taking her plate, he asked prosaically, 'Now what about some coffee?'

'I'd love some.'

'It won't keep you awake?'

Watching him fill two cups, she said, 'I doubt if anything could do that. In fact if I stay here much longer I'll go to sleep sitting up.'

The moment their coffee was finished, he relieved her of her cup and held out both hands to pull her to her feet.

'Goodnight.' Her face soft, she smiled at him.

'Goodnight.' As if it was the most natural thing in the world, he leaned forward to touch his lips to hers. His caress, though far from tentative, was sweet, gentle, posing no threat.

Like someone in a dream she returned his kiss, before turning to move away.

As she took a step his arms went around her and drew her back against him. Cassandra gave a soft gasp as his lips brushed the warmth of her nape, but made no effort to resist, and she heard his faint sigh.

She could feel the hard length of his body against her spine as, a hand beneath her chin, he tilted her head back against his shoulder while his mouth covered hers again.

His kiss brought a glow of warmth and pleasure, a stir of excitement. When his hands moved to rest lightly on her ribcage, his thumbs just brushing the undersides of her breasts, she felt no sense of fear, just a kind of breathless anticipation.

Her lips were parted beneath his, her body boneless, pliant in his embrace. Having deepened the kiss, he lifted his hands to cup her breasts.

As though held in thrall she made no protest, and when his lean fingers began to tease the sensitive nipples though the thin fabric of her dress she shuddered in response.

While his hands pleasured her, his mouth moved to

caress her throat and the soft skin beneath her jaw, sucking and nibbling, enticing and erotic.

He felt her body grow heavy and languid, and thought that making love to this woman was going to be not only a great deal easier than he'd expected, but a great deal more enjoyable.

There was something about her that excited him, an air of naivety, a lack of worldliness. She seemed to have the kind of purity he'd once hoped to find.

But common sense told him she couldn't be that pure. He knew she'd had at least two lovers. Yet all his male instincts insisted that she wasn't very experienced and, even more surprising, that in spite of her receptiveness she would be easily scared.

So for the moment he would keep a tight rein on his self-control, take things slowly and make sure he didn't allow the sensual spell she was under to slacken.

When he had made her molten with liquid heat, dazed with longing, when it was far too late for second thoughts, then would be the time for passion and urgency and delight...

Cassandra surfaced slowly, languorously, her brain still half stupefied by sleep, her body as sleek and contented as a well-fed cat. She was lying on her back, the silken sheets cool and voluptuous against her naked flesh.

Why wasn't she wearing her nightdress? she wondered blearily as, yawning, she opened heavy lids.

The strange room was dim apart from a single sliver of sunshine which slanted through a crack in the velvet curtains. It lay like a fairy's bright wand across a jumble of discarded clothes, amongst them her own cocktail dress, and a man's evening shirt and black bow-tie.

What on earth...?

Before the question was even completed, memory supplied the answer and set her heart racing with suffocating speed.

Jerking bolt upright, a mass of silky hair tumbling around her bare shoulders, she turned her head. Apart from herself the king-sized bed was empty. But someone had undoubtedly slept beside her.

No, not someone. *Lang Dalton.*

With instant and complete recall came total and utter disbelief. She *couldn't possibly* have slept with Lang Dalton. A man she'd known for less than forty-eight hours. A man she didn't love, and wasn't even sure she liked.

No, she couldn't, *wouldn't* believe it! She must be still asleep, trapped in some kind of bad dream.

But the cold voice of reason insisted that she was wide awake, and this was no bad dream she would eventually escape from.

Deeply shocked, shaken to the core, she was forced to face the unthinkable fact that Lang Dalton had succeeded in seducing her.

But how had he managed to get through not only her normal defences, but through the *involuntary* defences that even the man she loved had been unable to penetrate?

The uncomfortable answer came swiftly. A lethal combination of tiredness and too much to drink had to be to blame. As well as stupefying her mind it must have freed her repressions and inhibitions, and her own body, deprived for too long of its natural needs, had turned traitor.

She desperately *wanted* to blame Lang Dalton for what had happened. But it simply wasn't true that he had seduced her. She had been an equal partner, she recalled with a kind of awe. When he had kissed her, she had kissed him back. She had wanted him as much as he'd wanted her.

Even so, if he had been clumsy or tried to rush or force her in any way, it would have brought back all the old nightmare and made her afraid. But he had been very clever. Cool and unhurried. Sweet and seductive. Never putting a foot wrong.

Rather than his strength, he had shown her his need, made love to her with care and tenderness, a restrained passion that had evoked an answering passion.

A passion that had swiftly become white-hot. A passion that had taken most of the night to expend…

She had never suspected the sensual aspect of her nature that had lain dormant, buried first beneath an inbuilt shyness and insecurity, and later beneath an icy weight of stress and fear.

During that abortive weekend in Paris, her inability to respond to Alan, to become the warm and willing partner he'd been expecting, had almost ruined their relationship.

In desperation she had been forced to tell him about Sean to try and make him understand.

Clearly shocked, he'd asked sharply, 'Have you told anyone else in the office about this?'

'Not a soul. It isn't the kind of thing I'd want to talk about.'

His relief obvious, he'd advised, 'I think you should keep it that way. People might…well…misunderstand.'

Once the first shock had worn off, Alan had done his best to treat the whole thing practically.

Clearing his throat, he'd begun a shade pompously, 'I'm sure you don't regard me as a lustful man?'

'No.' In truth, anything but. It had been his lack of libido that had first drawn her to him. She had felt safe, under no pressure.

'But I do have certain needs. Needs that, now that I'm engaged, I feel I can't satisfy elsewhere…'

That point made, he went on, 'The house my parents left me will soon be available, so perhaps the sensible thing would be to bring our marriage forward. Once you're my wife and can put the past behind you, it will make all the difference. I'm sure I'm right.'

She'd nodded, and said with forced cheerfulness, 'Yes, I'm sure you are.'

But, badly shaken by her own lack of response, what she'd seen as her failure as a woman, she had begun to worry in case she really was the frigid bitch Sean had called her.

Now she knew she was anything but frigid, and if the circumstances had been other than they were that knowledge would have come almost as a relief, she thought wryly.

The moment Lang Dalton had begun to make love to her she had forgotten everything, her pride and self-respect, her doubts and fears, even the fact that she was engaged to another man. A man she loved and had promised to spend the rest of her life with.

She was filled with the most appalling guilt and shame. How could she ever face him again? How could she ever face *either* of them?

Cassandra groaned aloud. She had dreaded this weekend, but never in her worst nightmares had she imagined herself ending up in Lang Dalton's bed.

His bed. His room. He could walk in at any moment.

Galvanized into action by the thought, she pushed back the bedclothes and leapt out of bed, her bare feet sinking into the deep-pile carpet.

Pulling on a short maroon silk robe that had been tossed over a chair, she tied the belt with shaking hands. The sleeves were far too long and the shoulders buried her, but at least it covered her nakedness.

Breathlessly she gathered up her clothes and, clutching them to her chest, flung open the door into the living-room. To her utmost relief it was deserted.

As though the devil himself were at her heels she fled into her own room and turned the key in the lock. Then thought with bitter irony that such a precaution had come far too late. It was akin to shutting the stable door after the horse had well and truly bolted.

Her spirits heavy as a lead balloon, she went into the bathroom to brush her teeth and shower. Catching sight of herself in the mirror, she was surprised to see that apart from a certain paleness she looked just as usual, her face innocent, her green eyes clear.

But what had she expected? That she would look different? Like a scarlet woman?

She stepped into the shower and, as though trying to wash away all traces of the previous night, let the hot water flow over her for much longer than necessary, before drying herself.

Lang Dalton had been a gentle, considerate lover, and though her slender body *felt* subtly different her clear, healthy skin bore no signs of the passion that had flared between them.

Shivering at the thought, she put on an oatmeal-coloured sleeveless cotton dress and a pair of strappy sandals, and was just about to coil her hair into its usual neat chignon when there was a knock at the outer door.

Momentarily she froze, then common sense told her that the owner of the suite wouldn't need to knock. Letting the ash-brown silky mass tumble around her shoulders, she went to open the door.

'Hi!' Rob smiled at her. 'Lang said he'd left you still fast asleep. He asked me to escort you to lunch if he wasn't back in time.'

Flustered by Rob's casual acceptance of the implied intimacy, she said a shade stiffly, 'Thanks, but there's really no need. You must have plenty to do without being detailed off to play nursemaid.'

Choosing to ignore the slight bite in her words, he said cheerfully, 'I must admit I hadn't regarded it in quite that light... As far as I'm concerned there's nothing I'd rather do than sit opposite a beautiful woman over lunch... Especially as I hate eating alone.' The last was added with a rueful grin that in spite of everything had her smiling back.

Though she suspected that he was being diplomatic, she warmed to his charm, and, unwilling to hurt his feelings, gave in gracefully. 'Well, in that case...'

Instead of taking the elevator down, as she'd expected, he led her across the foyer to French windows that opened on to a roof garden.

Alongside the wide, flagged terrace there was a Jacuzzi and a good-sized swimming pool and, beyond, an expanse of cool green lawn shaded by palms.

It was hot and sunny, with a cloudless sky the colour of lapis lazuli. Beyond the Las Vegas sprawl, she could see distant mountains, hazy and insubstantial, shimmering in the desert heat like a mirage.

Beneath a trellis of sweet-smelling vines a table had been set with a buffet-style lunch. A bottle of wine stood in a cooler, and next to it a large bowl of sun-kissed Californian peaches.

Rob pulled out a chair for Cassandra, and when she was settled took a seat opposite.

As if by magic a smartly turned out manservant appeared at his elbow.

Cocking a brow at Cassandra, Rob asked, 'Would you like anything hot? Steak, or enchiladas, perhaps?'

She shook her head. 'Just a little green salad and coffee, please.'

Rob nodded, and said, 'I'll have the same.'

The manservant disappeared round the side of the terrace, to return quite quickly with a bowl of crisp salad, a basket of warm rolls, and a pot of coffee.

Having filled their cups, he queried, 'Will that be all, Mr Laski?' His voice was quiet, educated.

'Yes, thanks, John.'

Watching him walk away, Cassandra helped herself to salad and a roll, and, her winged brows drawn together in a frown, remarked, 'His eyes are sad. He looks...I don't know...as if he's had troubles...'

'You're very astute. John was once a brilliant accountant working for a top firm. He had a nice home, a wife he adored, and a baby son.

'Then somehow he began to mix with the wrong crowd and got hooked on drink and drugs. He lost everything and narrowly escaped a prison sentence when they discovered he'd been ''borrowing'' money from the firm to pay for his addiction. Things went from bad to worse when his baby son died of meningitis. He blamed himself...

'Less than a year ago he was a drifter, a drop-out, a no-hoper. Lang found him unconscious on the sidewalk, brought him back here, sobered him up, and offered him a second chance. Which he had the sense to take.

'In the past ten months, with Lang's help, he's managed to wean himself off drink and drugs, and pretty soon he's planning to go home to Carson City. His wife still lives there, and he's hoping for a second chance.'

'Will she have him back, do you think?'

With a slight shrug, Rob admitted, 'It may not work out if she does. He still feels that in some way the child's death was his fault. That kind of loss can take some living with...

'Even Lang, who's the most stable of men, took Nina's death very badly. He's still cut up over it, and I'd begun to wonder if he'd ever look at another woman...

'One way and another he's had more than his fair share of grief. That's why I was so damn glad when he told me about you.'

At a loss, Cassandra began, 'I don't really know what—'

'Ah, talk of the devil...'

Catching her breath, she glanced round to see Lang coming towards them looking vital and attractive. He was dressed in stone-coloured trousers and a white cotton-knit shirt, a pair of Polaroid glasses pushed into the top pocket.

In some strange way the casual garb only served to accentuate his aura of power and authority, his cool air of command.

Put a man like Lang Dalton to sweeping a floor, she found herself thinking, and without effort he'd manage to look as if he owned not only the building, but the entire block.

Pausing by her chair, he smiled down at her, teeth gleaming white against his tan. 'Had a good sleep?'

Her composure, fragile as glass armour, shattered into a million pieces and she prayed for the ground to open and swallow her up.

Bending over, he brushed his lips against hers. Though his kiss was light as thistledown, his impact on her senses was devastating. Her whole body tensed and flooded with heat.

Through her pink-cheeked confusion she was aware that Rob had risen to his feet and was excusing himself.

At the same instant John appeared with a fresh cafetière and another cup, and asked, 'Is there anything special you'd like, Mr Dalton?'

'No, thanks, John, I'll stick with fruit and coffee.'

As the man walked away, Lang dropped into the chair Rob had just vacated, and queried, 'More coffee?'

She shook her head.

He filled his own cup and drank, watching her over the rim, his dark blue gaze assessing. 'I hope Rob's taken good care of you?'

When, unable to find her voice, she remained silent, he continued, 'I'm sorry I had to leave you to wake up alone. I'd have liked nothing better than to stay and make love to you all over again, but I had some arrangements to make...

'However, they haven't taken as much time as I'd expected, so we could still go back to bed if you—'

'I've no intention of ever being in your bed again,' she broke in hoarsely.

He raised a quizzical brow. 'I rather got the impression you enjoyed it?'

'Last night should never have happened.'

'Regretting it?'

'Of course I'm regretting it. The whole thing was a terrible mistake. If I hadn't been tired and had too much to drink...'

Wryly amused, he observed, 'I think there was a little more to it than that.'

There was a *lot* more to it, but, unable to come to terms with her own uninhibited response to the sexual chemistry between them, she strove to deny it.

His smile deepened and, filled with a burning shame, she covered her face with her hands. 'I don't know how I'm ever going to tell Alan.'

After a moment, his voice casual, Lang enquired, 'You've decided to tell him?'

Her hands dropped into her lap. Dully, she said, 'It wouldn't be fair not to when we're going to be married—'

'Then you're still hoping to marry him?' Lang broke in swiftly.

'If he'll have me, when he knows what's happened.'

Lang passed lean fingers over his smoothly shaven jaw. 'How do you think he'll take it?'

In truth, she didn't know.

Yesterday she had felt relatively confident, secure in Alan's love. But last night had marred and undermined their relationship, destroying her certainty and threatening their chance of happiness.

But surely, when he'd got over the shock, he wouldn't let one act of stupidity spoil their whole future together?

Her voice scarcely above a whisper, she admitted, 'He's bound to be surprised and shocked... Bitterly disappointed in me.'

'I gather it won't be the first time?'

'I—I don't know what you mean,' she faltered.

'You mentioned a visit to Paris. Wasn't he disappointed then? Didn't he go there expecting to be your lover?'

Her expression was answer enough.

'So why didn't you sleep with him?'

'How do you know I didn't?'

'Oh, come on!' He laughed as if genuinely amused, and watched her flush deepen. 'I admit to being surprised. A twenty-two-year-old virgin was the last thing I'd expected...'

And that was the truth. When he'd further discovered that she responded with a white-hot, passionate sensuality, he'd wondered *how* and *why* she'd kept both her previous would-be lovers at bay. There was something strange, something he hadn't taken into account.

'Don't you believe a woman should exercise her sexual freedom?'

Stung, she retorted, 'That's exactly what I did. Any woman should have the freedom to say no if she wants to.' A little wildly, she added, 'I chose to work and wait for love rather than just sex.'

'But you told me you loved Brent.'

'I do,' she said in a strangled voice.

'Yet even when you became engaged you still kept him at arm's length. Why?'

'Hasn't it occurred to you that I might have been holding out for a wedding ring?'

'Were you?'

Suddenly defeated, close to tears, she silently shook her head.

'That may be just as well.'

'You don't think he'll go ahead with the wedding?'

Lang put the ball back in her court. 'Do you?'

'I hope so... Alan loves me...' She needed to reassure herself.

'He *may* love you, but I strongly suspect that he loves

himself more. You've kept him dangling on a string, kept him waiting...'

She denied, 'It wasn't like that...' and was aware she sounded defensive.

As though she hadn't spoken, Lang went on, 'So he isn't going to like the idea of you falling into another man's hands like a ripe plum.'

Swallowing hard, she managed, 'If I explain the circumstances I think he'll understand how and why it happened.'

It didn't need her companion's sceptical, 'Do you?' to make Cassandra realize how very unlikely that was. She didn't *fully* understand herself.

His smile sardonic, Lang went on, 'And in the unlikely event of Brent being so wonderfully understanding, do you really think he'd ever be able to forgive and forget?'

Trying to sound sure, she said, 'I believe he'd try.'

'Even if he was willing to *try*, I doubt very much he'd succeed.'

'Are you suggesting I shouldn't tell him?'

'I was merely pointing out the consequences if you do.'

After a moment, a deep-rooted conviction of what was right made her say, 'But I couldn't possibly marry him *without* telling him. As my future husband he has a right to know.'

'Your honesty does you credit.' Lang's voice was cynical. 'Of course, if you decided *not* to go ahead with the wedding, that changes everything. There would be no reason to tell him.'

'But I *want* to go ahead with the wedding.'

His eyes narrowed against the glare, Lang looked at her thoughtfully. 'After everything that happened between us last night?'

Trying to avoid his penetrating gaze, she moved uncomfortably. 'It was just sex.'

'You mean as in a casual one-night stand?'

'Yes.'

'I had the impression it was more than that. It seemed to me we shared something rather rare and wonderful. Or don't you agree?'

Oh, yes, it had been wonderful! But she hadn't expected it to mean that much to a sophisticated man like Lang Dalton, and his words totally threw her.

When she failed to answer, he insisted, 'Think about it.'

Thinking about it was the last thing she wanted to do, but she was unable to help herself; it was all there in her mind.

She recalled his lean, tanned body flexing over hers, bringing a delight she had never even dreamt of, while he told her of his own pleasure in words that heightened the exquisite eroticism of the act...

And, above and beyond that, a closeness, an intimacy that ordinary everyday communication could have taken weeks or months to achieve.

The kind of closeness that in the past she'd dreamt of. The kind of closeness it would be quite impossible to forget.

But somehow she would have to try.

Huskily, she repeated, 'It was only sex.'

'Well, don't knock it. Sex is an important part of life, and we have the right kind of chemistry, the vital spark that makes it good between us. Special.'

He smiled at her with such charm that her heart lurched and seemed to miss a beat, before picking up and starting to race.

Taking a deep breath, she countered, 'What makes you think it wouldn't be even better with Alan?'

'Because he's basically a cold fish...'

A *cold fish*... It was ironic that Alan had once described Lang in exactly the same terms.

'And selfish into the bargain.'

'How can you say that?' she cried indignantly. 'You don't really know him.'

'But I know the type, and I know how ready he was to put his own interests ahead of yours. Believe me, he's the wrong man for you. He's shallow and self-centred, incapable of caring deeply for anyone but himself.'

Desperately clinging to the rocks of sanity in a world where everything she had thought stable was shifting, she shook her head. 'I don't happen to think so. I love him. I want to be his wife, to enjoy the future we've planned together...'

Lang sighed. 'I thought you'd decided you couldn't marry him without telling him about last night? And if you do that you'll end up ruining any chance of happiness for either of you.'

'No!'

Ignoring her desperate protest, Lang went on, 'He'd find it impossible to forget that I've slept with his wife and he'd hate my guts.

'The mere fact that I'm his boss and always there in the background would make his position intolerable. He'd never feel able to trust either of us again. Every time his back was turned he'd wonder what we were up to.

'Eventually the strain would tell. Both his career and the marriage would fall apart...'

Knowing that Lang's assessment was probably only too true, she felt a bleak despair. How could she possibly inflict this on the man she loved?

'And we'd all end up losers—'

Her voice bitter, impeded, she broke in, 'I fail to see why you're including yourself.'

'I'd end up losing a valuable member of my workforce... But it goes without saying that the worst hit by far would be Brent; his entire life could well be wrecked.'

It was plain that Lang thought she should keep quiet, and perhaps, for Alan's sake, she should.

Making up her mind, she said jerkily, 'Then I won't tell him.'

'If he's expecting a virgin bride, won't he start asking awkward questions?'

'I'll just have to take that chance...' And live with the guilt, she added silently.

'So you've made up your mind to marry him and hide the truth?'

'Thinking about it, I don't see what else I can do.' Something in Lang's expression made her add uneasily, 'It *is* what you want, isn't it?'

'Not at all. You admitted that as your future husband he has a right to know, and I agree. In fact if you try to go ahead with the wedding without saying anything I'll be forced to tell him myself.'

CHAPTER FIVE

TAKEN aback by what seemed to be Lang's volte-face, she gaped at him. 'But why? I don't understand... From what you've been saying I felt sure you didn't *want* me to tell him...'

But even as she spoke she realized she'd read it wrongly; that *wasn't* what he had been aiming for. 'You don't want me to marry Alan at all!' she burst out.

When Lang made no attempt to deny the charge, she demanded, 'Why? What possible difference can it make to you?'

'Apart from the fact that I think you'd be making a big mistake, you might be pregnant.'

'Pregnant?' Every drop of colour drained from her face, leaving her ashen.

'Unless you were protected?'

She shook her head mutely.

With brutal honesty he told her, 'Believing you to be experienced, I didn't take any precautions...'

Then he said decidedly, 'The last thing I want is another man bringing up my child. Not, I imagine, that Brent would care overmuch for the idea...'

He certainly wouldn't, she thought distractedly. After some discussion Alan had suggested that to give both their careers a chance they should wait at least five years before they even considered starting a family. Seeing she was reluctant to agree, he had said firmly that for the time being at least he would take all responsibility for family planning.

'So if you *are* pregnant...' Lang pressed.

A quick calculation told her she couldn't rule it out,

and unless they postponed the wedding—and what earthly reason could she give for doing that?—she wouldn't be sure until it was too late.

Then what would she do if she *was?*

Her stomach churning sickeningly, she finally admitted what perhaps she'd known all along, that last night's madness had made marrying Alan out of the question.

Having given her a moment to think about it, Lang went on, 'It seems to me that if you really *do* love him it would be kinder to say nothing about what's happened and simply end the engagement. At least he'd have his career left.'

'But what reason can I give for breaking things off? The wedding's less than a week away. All the arrangements have been made...'

'Don't worry about arrangements; they can be cancelled. Just tell him you've changed your mind. You've realized in the nick of time that you're not suited and it would be a mistake.'

Miserably, she said, 'He'll be so hurt.'

'It's my belief he'll soon get over it.'

'You're a callous devil,' she muttered.

Lang's smile was mocking. 'Last night at one point you seemed to think I was altruistic.'

'Obviously I was mistaken,' she cried furiously, jumping to her feet. 'You don't give a damn that you've helped to wreck Alan's life.' She choked back a sob. 'I wouldn't put it past you to change your mind about his promised promotion...'

The strong jaw tightened. 'I don't recall *promising* him anything. *If* the promotion goes through is the way I phrased it.'

Suddenly afraid of this man, of the power he wielded, she muttered, 'Yes, I—I'm sorry...'

'As a matter of fact I had already decided *not* to give Brent the West Coast job.'

Lang studied her stricken face for a moment or two,

before adding, 'Would you feel any happier if I told you that I might be prepared to make him the overall head of European Finances?

'He would be based in Switzerland, which I gather he likes. When he first came to work for me he spent a year there, and transferred to London with some reluctance.'

Yes, Alan had once told her how much he'd enjoyed living in Switzerland. 'That would be wonderful—' A sudden realization made her break off abruptly. 'You said *might*...'

The dark blue eyes met and held hers. 'It all depends on you... If you agree to what I want, the post's his.'

'And if I don't?'

Lang said wryly, 'Let's presume you will.'

Her mouth desert-dry, she asked, 'What *do* you want?'

Leaning back in his chair, he smiled a little, while his leisurely gaze travelled over her slender body. 'Surely you know?'

'I won't be your mistress, if that's what you mean.'

He surprised her by saying, 'It isn't.'

'Then what...?'

'Please sit down...' Though politely phrased it was clearly an order.

When she sank back on to the chair, he went on calmly, 'Bearing in mind that you might possibly be pregnant, I think we should get married.'

'Married? No... No! I couldn't possibly marry you.' Panic-stricken, she sought for convincing reasons. 'We've only just met... I—I hardly know you...'

'In one way at least you know me a great deal better than you know Brent,' he pointed out with cool logic.

Watching him pick up a velvety peach and begin to quarter it, she protested wildly, 'But I don't love you.'

'I don't see that as a problem,' he said, unmoved. 'You know I can keep you satisfied in bed, and I'm a wealthy man; I can give you a great deal more than Brent ever could.'

'Do you think I give a damn for you or your money?' Her voice broke. 'I wish I'd never set eyes on you. I could have been *happy* with Alan.'

His smile crooked, Lang murmured, 'I must beg leave to doubt it. Does your heart beat faster when he looks at you? Do you tremble when he touches you?

'At the best your lovemaking would be tepid. You'd never burn for him like you burnt for me. Once he's out of your life and we're married you may even get to love me.'

'I won't marry you, and I'll *never* love you. I love Alan. He's all I care about...'

'I'm beginning to doubt it. If that were true you'd want to make it up to him, to see him get to the top of the tree.'

'I do.'

She watched Lang's white, healthy teeth bite through a segment of peach before, taking her by surprise, he leaned forward to pop the remaining piece in her mouth. 'Then it's up to you.'

Peach juice dribbled down her chin and she wiped it away with her napkin. 'I won't be forced to marry someone I hate the sight of just to get Alan a promotion!'

'There's rather more to it than that.'

A silken noose tightening around her slender throat, she breathed, 'You mean you'll get rid of him if I don't?'

Lang looked at her through thick, dark blond lashes. 'He certainly won't be working for me any longer.'

'Well, he's good at his job. He's bound to get other chances.'

'Believe me, there'll be no other chances. He'll be finished.'

'How can you know that?'

'I'll make certain of it.' There was a cold finality about the words that, despite the hot sun, caused a shiver to run through her.

Spiritedly, she said, 'I can't imagine even you have

the power to stop Alan succeeding with some other firm.'

'There aren't too many firms willing to give a man who's been jailed for embezzling a top post in their finance department.'

Failing to understand, she protested, 'But he *hasn't* been jailed for embezzling.'

'Not yet.' It was a threat. 'But fraudulently diverting money to one's own use is a serious crime.'

Aghast, she cried, 'I don't believe he's done any such thing.'

'No, he hasn't,' Lang agreed pleasantly. 'But I've contrived to make it *appear* that he has.

'If the London accounts that Brent's responsible for are carefully scrutinized they will show that quite a lot of money is missing.'

Cassandra pressed slim fingers against her temples. To set up something like that, Lang would have needed not only an accountant, but someone he could trust, someone who wouldn't give away his secret...

'I don't believe it,' she cried hoarsely. 'You're just bluffing.'

Not a whit disturbed, he invited, 'If you think that, call my bluff and see...'

She was wondering if she dared, when all at once she remembered Rob saying 'John was once a brilliant accountant...' *And obviously John owed Lang a big debt of gratitude.*

'If the accounts are examined and I'm forced to press charges,' Lang went on, 'when Brent gets out of prison—'

Desperately she broke in, 'I don't believe he could be convicted of something he didn't do.'

The broad shoulders moved in a slight shrug. 'Even if he was fortunate enough to get off, you know how mud sticks. After the media got hold of it, and I'd make sure they did, he'd be lucky to be offered a job as an office boy.'

White to the lips, she whispered, 'No! You can't do that to him. He's done nothing to deserve it.'

'Oh, I agree. And I hope it won't be necessary. But if you force my hand...'

'I could tell everyone what you've just told me,' she threatened wildly.

He laughed softly, derisively. 'Do you think anyone would believe you? Apart from the fact that you're Brent's fiancée, doesn't it sound just a tad too far-fetched and melodramatic?'

Of course it did, she acknowledged bleakly. Who would credit that a man like Lang Dalton would need to go to those lengths to force a woman to marry him?

In fact it just didn't make sense...

'And suppose you are pregnant,' he pursued. 'If you don't marry me what will you do? Have an abortion?'

Startled, she said, 'No, I'd never do that.'

'It wouldn't be easy bringing up a child alone.'

'Plenty of other women do it.'

'Have you considered that as it would be my baby as well I'd have some say in the matter? If you refused to marry me I might decide to take it from you.'

Startled, she asked, 'Would you want a child?'

His face curiously tight, he said, 'I've always wanted a family.'

Feeling as though she was sinking into quicksand, she said, 'But there's a good chance that I'm *not* pregnant.'

'Well, I've no intention of waiting to see. Either way I want my ring on your finger without delay.'

Reaching across the table, he took her hand. 'So what's your answer? Are you going to marry me?'

After his first marriage had ended so tragically, why on earth would he want to risk any chance of future happiness by marrying a woman he didn't love, and who didn't love him?

She snatched her hand away. 'I don't understand *why* you want to marry me... And *don't* mention sex...'

Blue eyes laughing, he said, 'I wouldn't dare.'

Ignoring his amusement, she battled on, 'I'm sure there are dozens of women who would be prepared to keep you happy in bed...'

'Oh, I'm sure you're right,' he agreed with mock gravity. 'But I don't happen to want a succession of bed-partners. I want a wife.'

'There must be plenty who would be only too pleased to marry you.'

'But not you?'

'No,' she said tightly.

He sighed. 'Pity. From the moment I set eyes on you it was—'

'Don't tell me it was love at first sight!' she scoffed.

'You don't believe in such a thing?'

'No, I do not! Love is something that has to grow.'

'Then we'll just have to give it some other name.'

'Try calling it lust,' she said sharply. *That* she was forced to believe in.

'Whatever you call it, no other woman will do. It's *you* I want and I'm prepared to go to any lengths to get you.'

'Even to the extent of framing an innocent man?'

'Do you doubt it?' His smile was as glittering and dangerous as a knife blade.

She had no doubt that he *could* be ruthless...

But if she said *no* and simply walked away, would he really go through with it? Deep down what kind of man was he? When she'd asked him if he was a gambler, he'd answered 'I have been known to play for high stakes, but only when the odds are stacked in my favour.'

Well, he'd made certain that the odds *were* stacked in his favour. So what if the gamble still failed? Somehow she couldn't see him being either petty or vindictive...

But for Alan's sake she dared not risk it...

Yet how could she tie herself to a man she didn't love?

With a kind of desperation, she said, 'Suppose I agree to be your mistress for as long as you want me?' It would be the lesser of two evils.

'Much as I appreciate the offer,' he said with smooth mockery, 'I'm afraid it won't do. As I've already made clear, I want you for my wife, and I've gone to a great deal of trouble to achieve that end.'

I've gone to a great deal of trouble to achieve that end...

The knowledge, the realization, that had been hovering on the periphery of her mind finally registered and crystallized into certainty.

Carefully, she said, 'A moment or two ago you mentioned seeing me for the first time—'

'And you refused to believe that what I felt was anything but lust.'

'Whatever you call it—' she echoed his earlier words '—is irrelevant. You threatened what would happen to Alan if I didn't marry you...'

Lang sat quite still, his blue eyes wary.

Triumphantly, she went on, 'But it won't work. You saw me for the first time *just two days ago*. There's no way you could have set up that plot you described.'

'I'm afraid you're wrong.'

'I don't—'

'Not about the latter,' he broke in calmly. 'As you rightly surmise that took time and care to put into place. You're wrong in presuming I hadn't seen you until two days ago.'

While she stared at him, green eyes widening, he went on, 'I first saw you about a year and a half ago, when I was over in London—'

'But I didn't work for Dalton International then...'

Completely ignoring the interruption, he went on,

'During that trip I happened to be crossing Regent College campus and I caught sight of you.'

Feeling as though she was suffocating, she began to shake her head. 'I don't believe you. You're making it up.'

Feeling in a back pocket for his wallet, he produced a snapshot and handed it to her.

Her heart beating in slow, heavy thuds, she stared down at a close-up of two girls emerging from a building she recognized as one of the lecture halls at the college.

It was obviously winter and snow lay on the ground. Both figures were muffled in duffle-coats and scarves, but were clearly identifiable as Penny and herself.

'Satisfied?' Taking the snapshot from her, he put it back in his wallet.

Hoarsely, she said, 'I don't understand what prompted you to take a photograph of two unknown girls.'

After a brief hesitation, he shrugged. 'When I'm in London I tend to behave like a tourist. I happened to have a camera with me, and it was a spur of the moment thing…'

She found his explanation, though glib, difficult to believe.

'Later I made a few enquiries and discovered who you were.'

There was a pause while she steadied herself and thought about what she'd learnt, before she said slowly, 'Then it wasn't just *chance* that when I graduated I was offered a job with Dalton International?'

'No, it wasn't just chance,' he admitted. 'Though at that point I had no particular plans, I couldn't get you out of my mind, and I didn't want to lose sight of you…'

That, to all intents and purposes, was the truth. Only later, when he was free, had he decided exactly what he was going to do.

'You'd been working for me about six months when

you were offered a job interview with another company…'

How on earth had he known that?

'It occurred to me that you might move on. You'd done very well at college, and I thought you were ambitious…'

'So you told Alan to make me his PA.'

'Exactly. Though I could have cheerfully broken his neck when he made you his fiancée as well…'

Feeling dazed, she wondered, Was it possible for a man who was supposedly happily married to lust after another woman?

'I knew I'd have to do something about it,' Lang went on, 'but the time wasn't right, so I was forced to leave things for a while.'

'But why did you leave it until a bare week before the wedding?'

He made a grimace. 'A slip-up, I'm afraid. Brent told me you were planning to get married next spring. If my information source hadn't mentioned the change of plan it might have been too late.'

'I wish to God it had been,' she muttered.

'It would have made the whole thing a great deal more difficult if he'd been your husband rather than your fiancé, but I would still have found some way to take you from him.'

Though the words were spoken lightly, she could sense the steely purpose behind them, and despite the heat a shiver ran up and down her spine.

'When I discovered the wedding had been brought forward, I knew I couldn't afford to wait a day longer. My main fear was that you might be pregnant. If you had been having a baby it would have posed real problems…'

That was an understatement. It would have meant the end of all his plans. Bitter as he was, there was no way he could have gone ahead if she'd been carrying Brent's child.

'It was a great relief when you assured me you weren't, and an added and unexpected bonus to find you hadn't even slept with him.'

She swallowed hard, feeling cold and panicky and slightly sick. The strange premonition that had made her feel both scared and threatened, that had made her so reluctant to meet Lang Dalton, had proved to be only too accurate.

Yet it was still difficult to believe so much had been simmering beneath the surface without her ever suspecting. Almost *impossible* to believe that in this modern world a free, independent woman could be coerced into marrying a man she didn't love and didn't want to marry.

Glancing at his watch, Lang said briskly, 'Now it's getting on for three o'clock, so I'm afraid I must press you for an answer.

'If it's yes, we'll be married straight away and Brent will get his promotion. If it's no…' He let the sentence tail off. 'Though I'm sure it won't come to that.'

His quiet confidence shook her, as it had been meant to, yet still she fought a rearguard action. 'How long do you imagine a marriage like that could possibly last?'

His voice inflexible, he answered, 'If you happen to be pregnant, you might choose to stay with me. If not, then as long as I want it to last.'

How could something so bizarre have happened to her through no fault of her own? And the worst of it was, she wasn't alone. Poor Alan, caught up in all this, equally innocent and unsuspecting, stood to lose everything. Perhaps be branded a jailbird.

No, she couldn't let that happen. She owed him a big debt of gratitude. He was the only person who had ever loved her, and she would never be able to live with herself if she let him suffer for it.

Watching her face like a hawk, judging his moment, Lang took both her hands and, his previous hardness replaced by a reassuring gentleness, asked, 'Well?'

'What about the missing money?' she asked raggedly. 'Do you intend to keep that threat hanging over Alan's head?'

'No. The moment you say yes, I'll make arrangements to have the money replaced, and all traces of fraudulent conversion removed from the books.'

Staring down at the lean, tanned hands holding hers, and the muscular wrists where a sprinkling of sun-bleached hairs glittered, she agreed tonelessly, 'Very well, I'll marry you.'

Drawing her to her feet, he said jubilantly, 'Then let's go and get changed.'

'For what?' she asked as he hurried her across the terrace and through the door into the penthouse.

'For our wedding. Everything's organized...'

So they were the 'arrangements' he'd been making. He must have been very sure of her, she thought bitterly.

'The chapel's booked for four-thirty, and as I wanted to avoid the more tacky places it's a reasonable drive out of town.'

He'd said 'straight away', but she hadn't realized he'd meant it quite so literally. 'Oh, but I need to talk to Alan first. I have to try and explain—'

A shade impatiently, Lang broke in, 'It would be almost impossible to explain without telling him the truth. And I presume you don't want to do *that*, as it would defeat the object?'

She shook her head. 'No, I—'

'Then talking about it would be both harrowing and futile. The best way would be to say as little as possible. Simply face him with a *fait accompli*.'

'It would be such a shock...'

'But kindest in the long run.' Lang's expression said that the matter was now closed.

Turning her towards her bedroom door, he gave her a little push. 'You've got exactly fifteen minutes to put on your wedding dress and get ready, unless you want me to come looking for you... Oh, and leave your hair down.'

Like someone in a dream she went into her room and closed the door behind her. On the bed was a large ivory box.

Opening it with unsteady hands, she found, swathed in soft tissue paper, a halter-neck, knee-length dress of blue silk chiffon shot with the delicate pinks and greens and golds of a desert sky at sunset.

It needed no bra, but with it were a pair of dainty briefs and a half-slip, a matching stole, and pair of high-heeled sandals.

Lang, it seemed, had thought of everything.

The outfit, obviously chosen with great care, was lovely and romantic. For some unaccountable reason, her eyes filled with tears and she was forced to blink them away.

If only he really had loved her, in spite of everything they might have made it work. But all he felt for her was a kind of weird attraction, and all she felt for him was...

What did she feel for him? She should hate him after the way he'd wrecked her life, but all she could feel at this moment was exhausted and empty, utterly drained.

The only thing she wanted to do was crawl into bed, close her eyes, and find the blessed oblivion of sleep.

But she couldn't do that. She had a bare fifteen minutes to get ready, and she didn't intend to have him come looking for her. The only way she could face what lay ahead would be with spirit and dignity, and as much pride as she could muster.

That decision taken, she hurried into the bathroom and, stripping off her clothes, pulled on a shower cap and stepped under the spray of hot water.

Fifteen minutes later, she was dressed and ready. Trembling inside, cool and composed on the outside, she walked into the sitting-room with her back ramrod-straight and her head held high.

To show she didn't mean to obey him slavishly, her hair had been tamed into a businesslike chignon.

Lang rose to his feet and came to meet her. His dark blond hair was still a little damp from the shower, and he'd changed into a well-cut lightweight suit and tie. He looked tough and handsome and disturbingly attractive.

He took both her hands, and his critical gaze travelled over her from head to toe. 'You make a beautiful bride. But I don't think you need this.' He removed Alan's ring, which she had deliberately left on her finger as a further gesture of defiance, and slipped it into his pocket.

'Nor do we need the "Secretary Marries Boss" look.' Before she could make any protest he was deftly removing the pins from her hair.

'That's better,' he said as the silky mass tumbled around her shoulders.

'Quite sure you're satisfied?' she asked tartly.

'Not yet,' he said blandly, 'but I expect to be.'

Cheeks burning, she wished she'd stayed silent.

From a Cellophane box on the sideboard he removed an exquisite spray of small, delicate green and gold orchids, pale pink rosebuds, blushing magnolias and creamy carnations all interlaced with pale blue and green ribbon. 'Your bouquet.'

Their combined scent was sweet and heady, not unlike freesias, and she knew she would never smell anything like it again without reliving this moment.

'Just one more thing…' Seemingly from nowhere he produced a ring with a huge sparkling emerald in a plain gold setting, and slipped it on to her engagement finger. It fitted perfectly and looked wonderful on her slim but strong hand.

Though she knew very little about gems she could tell it was an unusually fine stone, the colour clear and good.

When she made no comment, he remarked, 'I thought it would match your eyes, but if you prefer we can replace it with a diamond.'

She shook her head. 'I would be quite happy if I didn't have a ring.'

'Ah, but *I* wouldn't... Ready to go?'

'As ready as I'll ever be.'

At his quirked eyebrow, she added, 'Surely you don't expect me to appear ecstatic?'

'Not when we're alone.' An edge of steel to his voice, he added, 'But when there are other people present I shall expect you to make some effort to appear reasonably happy.'

Having laid it on the line, a hand at her waist, he escorted her to the door and across to the elevator.

When they reached the foyer it was deserted apart from two well-dressed elderly women sitting on a gilt-backed settee, and a smart young man behind the reception desk who looked up with a smile.

'The car's here, Mr Dalton. They've left it by the steps.'

He produced a bunch of keys, which Lang took with a nod and a word of thanks.

It wasn't the big four-wheel drive Cassandra had been expecting, but a sleek ice-blue convertible, its top down, sun glancing off its polished bonnet.

Taking her bouquet, he put it on the back seat and handed her the car keys. 'A present for you.'

When she just stood with her mouth open, he suggested, 'I thought you might like to drive?'

It was a far cry from the old Cavalier she drove in London, and while one part of her itched to get behind the wheel a feeling of outrage, that he thought he could sway her with presents, made her shake her head and give him back the keys. 'I really can't accept it.'

She saw his jaw tighten, but his voice was calm, reasonable, as he said, 'Don't you agree that a bridegroom should buy his bride a wedding present?'

'Even if she's been coerced into marrying him?'

Blue eyes dancing, he repeated what she'd said to him during their first conversation. '*Especially* if she's been coerced into marrying him.'

Refusing to be won over by his undeniable charm, she informed him stiltedly, 'I would prefer not to have it.'

'And I would prefer not to have to send it back.' Once again she heard that hint of steel.

Almost pleadingly, she said, 'I don't want you to keep buying me things. I can't afford to lose my self-respect on top of everything else.'

'Perhaps, if you regard this as a one-off, we can *both* keep our self-respect.'

Signifying her surrender, she said, 'But I have nothing to give you.'

'Oh, I wouldn't say that,' he drawled, and smiled as her cheeks grew warm.

Vexed that he could so easily make her blush, when he offered her the keys, refusing to make her surrender total, she asked with cool hauteur, 'Will you drive?' A second later she spoilt the effect by adding, 'Despite the fact that I slept so late, I'm still rather tired.'

'Then we'll have an early night tonight,' he promised gravely as he opened the car door and helped her in.

Her blush deepening, looking anywhere but at him, she settled herself into the comfortable seat, and fastened her seatbelt.

He slid in beside her. A moment later the engine sprang into life with a soft, throaty purr, and they were off.

To her horror, his words had set her pulses racing and made every nerve-ending in her body tingle with anticipation. Damn him... Oh, *damn* him!

She could almost wish he was physically unattractive,

or a clumsy, insensitive, uncaring lover, then at least she would be able to remain unmoved and salvage her pride.

But she was forced to admit that he was none of those things. He was skilful and sensitive, caring and generous, and wildly exciting…

Snapping off the thought like a dry twig, she told herself sharply that if she wanted to retain any degree of composure the last thing she could let herself think about was the coming night.

CHAPTER SIX

SEEING him glance in her direction, aware she must look flushed and agitated, she turned away to stare resolutely out of the window.

They were driving through streets that in the afternoon heat were practically empty. It seemed that Las Vegas snoozed during the day and only blossomed into brilliant life after dark.

Now last night's ribbons of laser and neon had faded into insignificance, eclipsed by the bright sun, it looked even more unreal.

Remembering the instant wedding chapel she'd seen the previous evening, Cassandra felt a sudden distaste. This would be very different from the simple church wedding she had planned.

Though as it was a forced marriage to the wrong man, what did it matter? Maybe the very fact that it was so different would help to make it bearable...

But that sounded as though she had *accepted* the situation, whereas it still seemed inconceivable that she was about to become the wife of a man she hardly knew, and was closer to hating than loving.

Even when she had agreed to marry Lang, and put on what was to be her wedding dress, part of her mind had found it impossible to credit that it really was going to happen. She had felt a sense of disbelief, of unreality...

When they reached the edge of town, as though it had lain in wait like some playful animal, a hot desert wind sprang up.

It pounced on the fine sandy grit at the side of the unpaved road, swirling it into dust-devils, and bowled a tangle of dry and spiky vegetation along like tumble-weed, before ruffling Lang's thick blond hair and tossing Cassandra's tangle of loose curls.

Since they'd left the Golden Phoenix neither of them had spoken, each busy with their thoughts. Now, slanting her a glance, Lang broke the silence to remark, 'Soon be there.'

A moment or two later a sprawl of pastel-washed buildings came into view. Amongst them were several places to eat, some turn-of-the-century shops, and a saloon with a wooden railing and boardwalk.

The scene was charming and colourful, with bougain-villaea-draped walls and several varieties of cacti flowering in brilliant profusion. A few people were wandering about, but most of them looked like tourists, rather than locals.

In the centre of the village, in a dusty, sun-baked square, stood a little white chapel with narrow windows and adobe walls. Simple and picturesque, Spanish in style, its bell was sharply outlined against a cloudless, cornflower-blue sky.

'This is it,' Lang remarked, bringing the car to a halt beneath the shade of an old, gnarled tree.

Surprised, she admitted, 'It isn't a bit what I'd expected.'

'Although the Chapel of San Miguel is still used for "instant weddings" it's somewhat better than average. There are no plastic flowers or highly scented candles, no guitar-playing Elvis look-a-likes singing "Love me Tender", and no warm "champagne".'

Jumping out, he came round to open the door and help her out, before handing her her bouquet.

Looking around, wanting to buy a little time, she asked, 'Is this a genuine, lived-in village, or some kind of tourist attraction?'

'It used to be lived in, but now it's just a showplace

for tourists to visit, I'm afraid. Though of its kind, it's quite well done.'

Taking her hand, he tucked it under his arm and led the way towards the chapel. At the old, sun-warmed doors they were met and greeted by a slim, petite, no longer young woman, wearing a fawn suit and a trim white blouse with a bow at the neck.

Though Lang had made it clear that this was still essentially a Las Vegas-type wedding, Cassandra had half expected a black-frocked priest.

Smiling pleasantly, the woman queried, 'Mr Dalton and Miss Vallance? I'm Emmaline Veras... How nice to meet you.' She shook hands with them both.

Then, obviously used to dealing in practicalities, she suggested to Cassandra, 'As you're wearing an engagement ring, it might be a good idea to move it over to your other hand.'

The swap duly made, she led the way inside. 'Everything's ready for you. Mr and Mrs Lopez will act as your witnesses.'

Smiling, the witnesses rose from the back pew where they'd been waiting. Mr Lopez was wearing a flower in his buttonhole. All four shook hands before the bridal pair moved on.

The chapel was cool and dim after the glare, with rough white-plaster walls and a plain wooden altar. An equally plain wooden cross was flanked by twisted, black metal candlesticks.

When they reached the altar steps, obeying a sudden impulse, Cassandra put her bouquet down on the front pew and, pulling free a single carnation, turned to put it in Lang's buttonhole.

As they stood facing each other, their eyes met and held. Some emotion she was unable to decipher flared in his, before he lifted her hand to his lips and kissed the palm.

How long they stood there gazing into each other's

eyes before Emmaline Veras cleared her throat to gain
their attention, Cassandra never knew. But when she tore
her gaze away from Lang's she felt oddly giddy and
light-headed.

A moment later the ceremony began. Though it was
very short and to the point, the age-old, solemn phrases
were still used and still held meaning.

'Do you take...? With this ring...'

Like someone in a dream Cassandra listened to Lang's
responses, made her own, and watched him produce a
plain gold ring which he slid on to her finger.

A few moments later it was all over.

'By the authority invested in me... Man and wife...
You may kiss the bride.'

Lang's kiss, though light, was proprietorial enough to
leave her breathless and shaken.

After more handshakes and thanks all round, Lang
passed a discreet but, Cassandra guessed, liberal gratuity
to the witnesses, and they made their way to the door.

Outside, a battered pick-up had been parked next to
the convertible, and a young couple, little more than
teenagers, were standing in the hot sun waiting.

The bride-to-be was wearing a new and pretty, but
obviously inexpensive, dress, in shades of pink and blue.
She carried no flowers.

Cassandra glanced at Lang who, apparently reading
her thoughts, gave an almost imperceptible nod.

As the pair approached, she invited, smiling, 'Catch,'
and tossed her bouquet.

The girl caught it, and smiled back. 'Congratulations.
I hope you'll both be very happy.' She made to return
the bouquet.

'Oh, please keep it,' Cassandra urged. 'I'd like you
to.'

'Thank you, it's *beautiful*.' The girl's face flushed
with pleasure. Frankly, she added, 'Pete and I decided
that instead of spending what little money we had on

flowers we'd have a special meal out tonight to celebrate.'

'Then perhaps, as a wedding present, you'd allow us to contribute a bottle of champagne?' Unobtrusively. Lang passed the fresh-faced bridegroom a folded bill.

He was rewarded by an earnest, 'Gee, thanks! This sure is turning out to be our lucky day!'

The pair smiled joyfully at each other and, holding hands, moved forward to be greeted by Emmaline Veras. Cassandra sighed, envying their obvious happiness. They looked so elated, so sure of themselves and their love for each other. Whereas she was full of doubts and fears, of anger and resentment, of anxiety over the present—she still had to think of some way to break the news to Alan—and dread of the future.

Watching her expressive face, Lang lifted a level brow. 'Bad as that?' Though his tone was mocking, his expression showed genuine understanding, perhaps even a hint of sympathy.

'What time is Alan due back?' she asked baldly.

'Not until late this evening.'

Having handed her into the car, Lang got in beside her and went on, 'We've plenty of time for a sightseeing drive, and then a celebratory meal of our own, if that suits you?'

About to tell him *she* had nothing to celebrate, Cassandra paused. She'd agreed to the marriage—rather than chance calling his bluff—so for everyone's sake she would have to try and make the best of it. There was no point in making a bad situation worse by being openly morose or miserable.

Determinedly shrugging aside all her woes, she agreed, 'That sounds fine.'

'In spite of all the development going on around Las Vegas, there's still some wonderful country close at hand... Or if you prefer, rather than a drive, we can go to a town where there are shops, and things going on?'

'I'd much prefer to take a drive.' She chose without hesitation.

Remembering her enthusiasm for the journey to Nevada, he asked, 'You really like desert country?'

She gave him a sudden impish grin. 'Despite what I said earlier, I can only describe it as love at first sight…'

This woman never failed to surprise him, Lang thought. Not only did she have warmth and courage, and a sense of fun, but the things she seemed to enjoy didn't fit in with the kind of nature he'd expected.

'Until now I've only ever seen this kind of terrain in Westerns,' she went on, 'and I'd like to see more of the real thing.'

'Well, ma'am.' With a slight grin, he flicked an imaginary stetson, moved his chaw tobacco from one cheek to the other, and drawled, 'You've sure come to the right place…'

Taken by surprise, Cassandra burst out laughing. She hadn't expected him to have a sense of humour.

'If you can think of anywhere in pertic'ler you'd like to eat, we'll mosey along in that direction…'

Following his lead, she fluttered her lashes at him. 'Why, Marshal Dalton, you don't mean I get to choose?'

Appreciating her mood swing, he answered laconically, 'Sure do, ma'am.'

Suddenly she saw the ideal way to disconcert him, to pay him back for the times he'd deliberately made her blush.

Hugging herself, she said with a look of wide-eyed innocence, 'Well, I've always wanted to eat at a real, all-American…burger bar.'

'You don't mean it?' He sounded half amused, half aghast.

'I sure do.'

Wondering how far his sense of humour would stretch, she held her breath and waited for the explosion.

But all he said was, 'If that's so we'll get started on

the drive.' Removing his jacket, he tossed it on to the back seat, and added calmly, 'In the meantime let me know if you change your mind.'

Well aware he'd been anticipating haute cuisine and champagne, she had confidently expected a downright refusal, or at the very least a strong and immediate attempt to dissuade her. But it seemed he was prepared to play a waiting game.

The extreme heat of the day was over and the temperature was pleasantly hot without being overpowering. Enough of a breeze still lingered to cool her cheeks and lift her hair.

Steadfastly closing her mind to everything but the immediate present, Cassandra found herself thoroughly enjoying the drive through spectacular country.

Something primitive and vital in her responded to the wide expanse of burning blue sky, the sudden outcrops of reddish rock, the fascinating flora and fauna, and the harsh, sun-bleached beauty of the desert terrain.

From time to time Lang stopped to point out some interesting cacti or bird, and the occasional lizard sunning itself on one of the smooth boulders.

Penny, who shared her passion for old Westerns, would have adored all this...

Cassandra hadn't realized she'd spoken the thought aloud until he queried, 'Who's Penny?'

'Penny Lane, the girl I share a flat with. You must have heard—?'

He gave her a sidelong grin. 'Yes, I have heard the old Beatles number... Have you known her for long?' he added casually.

'For years. She was my room-mate at college.'

'The whole time?'

'Yes. We took most of our classes together. During our final year we decided to move out of the student accommodation and get a flat together.'

Memory gave Cassandra a nudge, and a shade unevenly she added, 'Penny's the other girl in the snap-shot…'

Perhaps to cover an awkward pause, Lang asked, 'What does she do now?'

'She works for you, as a matter of fact. She's just joined the research department… Though she got *her* job fair and square.'

When he made no comment, Cassandra went on, 'Penny's a good friend: loyal, kind-hearted, totally honest, down-to-earth in many ways, but at the same time wildly romantic…

'She was expecting to be my bridesmaid. She chose a lovely silk dress, all ruched and decorated with rose-buds…' Cassandra's voice cracked. 'I'll have to tell her it won't be needed now.'

As she finished speaking, Lang brought the car to a halt to allow a rattlesnake to cross the road and slither into the safety of a pile of tumbled rocks.

By this time the sun had dipped towards the western horizon, and the black shadows cast by tree-like cacti had lengthened dramatically.

When the sky became flushed with pink and gold, and the first star appeared, they turned towards civilization and the bright lights.

Cassandra was waiting for him to either reopen the question of where they should eat, or simply choose what he considered a more suitable place, when he drew into a burger bar's car park and said, 'Well, here we are. Hungry?'

'Ravenous,' she admitted.

He set the electronic code which locked the steering wheel, and picked up his jacket. 'Then let's go, shall we?'

Still unsure whether or not he was joking, she allowed herself to be escorted inside. They found a table for two, and he hung his jacket over the back of a chair.

It was bright and clean and busy, filled mainly with

young families and teenagers, most of whom sported
way-out clothing and hairstyles. A lot of the men fa-
voured either pony-tails or shaved heads.

In smart trousers, a silk shirt and tie, and with a conventional haircut, Lang stood out from the crowd, but
he showed no sign of feeling out of place.

With unruffled good humour, and an aplomb she was
forced to envy, he joined one of several lengthy queues
to order at the counter.

Watching him apparently sharing a joke with a tat-
tooed youth in the neighbouring queue who, judging by
the number of rings through his lips, nose and eyebrows
was heavily into body-piercing, she marvelled.

The queues were moving fast, and it wasn't long before Lang was back with a crowded tray.

'No expense spared,' he said cheerfully, unloading
various boxes and cartons. 'Two chicken nuggets with
dips, two double cheeseburgers, two large fries, and two
coffees. Tuck in.'

Hoist with her own petard, she opened the nearest
carton and began. A second later he followed suit, using
his fingers and eating with apparent enjoyment.

'A somewhat unusual wedding feast,' he remarked
gravely when they'd finished. 'Still, it makes a nice
change... And no one could say the atmosphere isn't
friendly...'

Only the gleam in his eye told her he'd been quite
aware of her motive for suggesting the place, and was
enjoying having the last laugh.

'Now, would you like an ice cream, or more coffee?'

She shook her head.

'Then let's go.'

Expertly gathering up the debris, he tipped it all neatly
into one of the waiting bins and put the tray on top of
the stack.

As they made their way back to the car she had to
admit that Lang had won fair and square. He'd seemed

perfectly at home in what, for him, she had thought of as an alien environment.

But, recalling their stop at Minnie's Diner the previous night, she knew she had been completely wrong. Though a wealthy man, he was no snob.

Forced into the same situation, Alan would have been horrified. Somewhat narrow and conventional, always very aware of his image, he would have looked and acted like a fish out of water in either place.

Seeing the faint smile that touched her lips, her new husband queried, 'Would you like to share the joke?'

Knowing it would sound disloyal to Alan, she shook her head.

Lang didn't press her, and they got into the car and drove back to the Golden Phoenix in silence.

As they crossed the foyer on their way to his private elevator, Lang left her for a moment to have a quick word with the man on the desk.

It was still relatively early, and she noticed a number of well-dressed guests making their way into a luxuriously carpeted dining-room lit by several crystal chandeliers.

The contrast between that and their own dining experience could hardly have been wider.

Catching her eye, Lang grinned, and she knew he'd been thinking much the same.

When they reached their suite he swept her up into his arms and carried her over the threshold. Smiling into her surprised face, he kissed her lightly before setting her on her feet again.

A little breathlessly, she said, 'I didn't realize you were such a traditionalist.'

'It seemed fitting.'

When she looked at him blankly, she saw a gleam in his eye. He said, 'I understand the custom relates to when the Romans carried the Sabine women, reluctant brides indeed, into their homes,' and watched the colour creep into her cheeks.

A supper trolley was waiting, spread with a selection of cold delicacies and a pot of coffee keeping hot. In the centre, alongside a bottle of vintage champagne, was a wedding cake with a diminutive bride and groom holding hands beneath an icing-sugar arch.

A large congratulations card, signed by all the staff, had been propped against the ice bucket, and next to it was a personal card from Rob, wishing them every future happiness.

Discarding his jacket, Lang came over and slipped the stole from Cassandra's shoulders. 'Champagne or coffee?'

'Coffee, thank you,' she said with careful politeness. 'But first I'd like to freshen up.'

Nerves starting to tighten, she needed a moment to herself. While they were out and about, she had been able to keep the thought of the coming night at bay. Now they were back, it was a different matter.

Going through to her bathroom to wash her face and hands and brush her tangled hair, she discovered that all her belongings had vanished. Presumably moved into Lang's room.

Though the youth behind the desk hadn't appeared to notice, the news that she'd walked out carrying a bouquet must have spread like wildfire.

Yet even as the thought crossed her mind Cassandra felt certain there was more to it than that. She was all at once convinced that Rob, at least, had known in advance that they were to be married. It explained both the things he'd said to her and his manner. In fact he'd known before *she* did.

But, in retrospect, she could see that right from the start Lang had been at some pains to give Rob the impression that they were lovers. The fact that she'd been

wearing an engagement ring—which he must have presumed was Lang's—could only have added to the image.

It had been a risk, of course; at any minute she might
have mentioned Alan. But in the event it had worked
beautifully. The wedding had taken place and no one
had been unduly surprised.

Up till now. It might be a different matter when Alan
arrived...

When she got back to the other room, Lang was just
emerging from his own bedroom, looking fresh and vir-
ile, his thick blond hair neatly brushed.

Closing her mind to his appeal, she remarked
abruptly, 'You said Alan would be late...' Even to her
own ears her voice sounded strained. 'How late?'

Then she said with a rising resentment, 'You must
know. You planned the whole thing every step of the
way.'

Looking completely unruffled, Lang answered, 'He's
due to attend a top management dinner at Seguro House
before they start back, so he shouldn't be arriving just
yet... Why don't you sit down and relax while I get that
coffee?'

Feeling unable to do either at that minute, she remained standing, while he poured the steaming liquid
into two cups and handed her one.

As they sipped, she made a determined effort to stay
calm. Letting herself get het up would serve no useful
purpose. It would only make matters worse.

But try as she might she was unable to prevent her
mind jumping ahead to the inevitable scene with Alan.

How on earth could she tell him that in the short time
he'd been away she had married Lang Dalton?

And how badly would he take it?

She felt a momentary panic. What if Alan's feelings
ran a great deal deeper than either of them had suspected? In the ordinary run of things he wasn't a man
to indulge in grand gestures, but, faced with a situation

like this, suppose he was hurt and angry enough to sacrifice his career and walk out?

Lang had seemed so sure that he *would* accept the
promotion offered, and she had gone along with it... But
what if they were both wrong?

No, surely he wouldn't throw everything away, neither for the sake of his pride nor for her. She knew in
her heart of hearts that he had never viewed their engagement with half the eagerness and excitement with
which he had viewed his career.

If they had married, their relationship, she felt sure,
would have been placid rather than passionate. Alan
looked on passion in much the same way as he looked
on strong emotion of any kind, as something best
avoided...

And knowing where passion could lead, afraid and
wary, she had been only too pleased... Until last night...

'More coffee?' Lang's voice broke into her thoughts.

Shaking her head, she said jerkily, 'I keep wondering
what will happen... I mean, when Alan knows. What
will he do? Where will he go? He'll have to spend the
night somewhere and you can hardly expect him to...'
She tailed off helplessly.

'To stay under the same roof?' Lang finished for her.
'No, I'd already thought of that. So I've arranged to have
a car standing by to take him straight back to the airport,
where the company jet will be waiting for him.'

'And I suppose that's purely for *his* sake?' she demanded with some bitterness.

'No, it's for all our sakes,' Lang admitted calmly. 'I
thought, as tonight's our wedding night, you might find
it inhibiting to have him too close.'

Watching the colour rise in her cheeks, he went on,
'And when he knows the score I imagine he'll be only
too eager to leave for San Francisco as soon as possible.
That way he'll be able to return to England on tomorrow's scheduled flight, as planned.

'If he accepts the promotion, which I don't doubt he will...' there it was again, that arrogant certainty '...all the necessary arrangements have been made, so he can take up his new post in Switzerland as soon as he has a mind to.'

He made it appear very cut-and-dried and simple. But could human emotions really be dealt with in such a ruthlessly businesslike manner?

'Lang...when he does come...I'd like to break it to him as gently as possible.'

Sounding a shade more human, Lang admitted, 'It's bound to come as a shock, however it's done. He won't like the idea of losing out to another man. But it's something he'll have to come to terms with, and I don't see any point in beating about the bush.'

'No, but I can't bear the thought of—'

'Believe me,' Lang broke in crisply, 'it isn't my intention to cause either you or Brent any unnecessary pain. Just the opposite, in fact.'

Though far from satisfied with that assurance, she felt forced to let the matter drop.

Seeing how tense she was, Lang relieved her of the empty coffee cup, and chided softly, 'Take it easy; you look fraught.'

Moving behind her, he brushed aside her cloud of silky hair, and began to massage the taut muscles in her neck and shoulders. His hands were strong and well-shaped, with a touch that was both assured and delicate. Exciting hands...

Banishing the treacherous thought, she willed herself to relax, while his thumbs stroked and probed. After a minute or so some of the tension eased, and the dull ache at the back of her skull ceased.

Lightly holding her upper arms, he bent his head until his lips were brushing her ear, and queried, 'Better?'

'Yes, much better, thank you,' she answered huskily.

Then, feeling the smoothness of his jaw, she said, 'You've shaved.'

'Mmm…' He rubbed his cheek against hers. 'Bristles can be ruinous to a complexion like yours.'

His lips traced the whorls of her ear, and lingered on the warmth of her nape, making little shivers run through her.

As she stood in a kind of sensuous daze, he drew her back against his lean, muscular length and his hands moved to cover her breasts in a gentle, open-palmed caress, while his mouth travelled up the side of her neck to find the sensitive skin beneath her jaw.

Feeling her breathing and heart rate quicken perceptibly, he rubbed his thumbs lightly across her nipples and smiled when they firmed at his touch.

One hand continued the erotic stimulation while the other slid up her throat to tilt her head back against his shoulder. Her lips were soft and slightly parted, innocent as a child's.

His first kiss was light, almost chaste, touching and lingering, savouring the velvety softness. Then, with a sudden impatience, he turned her into his arms and, holding her face between his palms, lifted it to his.

A series of kisses, each less chaste than the last, made every nerve in her body leap into life and fire race through her.

At the mercy of feelings that were comparatively new and distinctly earth-shattering, she felt a sudden wild delight, a clutch of arousal that tightened the muscles of her abdomen into a knot and formed a core of liquid heat.

He knew, and between kisses he whispered deeply, 'Your body is so eager and vital, so responsive. Making love to you is like making love to a flame.'

While he continued to kiss her with passion and skill, lost to everything but the sensations he was so effortlessly arousing, she was scarcely aware that his deft fingers were unfastening the halter neck of her dress and sliding down the zip.

She only appreciated that she was naked to the waist when his hand moved to cradle the warm weight of her breast, and his mouth left hers to rove over the exposed curves.

He used the tip of his tongue to circle and stroke the dusky pink skin around the nipple before his mouth closed over the waiting peak.

The exquisite, needle-sharp sensations his suckling was causing brought a little whimper to her lips, an involuntary protest against sensual overload.

Yet when he made to draw away, suddenly bereft, she slid her fingers into the thick corn-silk of his hair and pulled his head down to hers.

While one hand roamed over her slender curves, he began to kiss her as though he was starving for her. With no thought of holding back, she clung to him, her arms around his neck.

His exploration of her mouth was thorough and unhurried and deeply sensual, the brush of his tongue against her lips utterly devastating.

Through a rising storm of desire she was aware of a knock, and a bare second later she heard the door behind her open.

Lang lifted his head and straightened, holding her protectively against him.

Hot with embarrassment, she expected an explosion of anger against whichever member of staff had dared to walk in without waiting for permission.

But in complete silence, his manner cool and unhurried, Lang proceeded to adjust her dress, pull up the zip, and fasten the halter neck. Then, his hands lightly gripping her upper arms, he turned her to face the intruder.

Transfixed in the doorway, his mouth open, his expression a study in stunned disbelief, Alan was standing as though turned to stone.

CHAPTER SEVEN

FOR what seemed an age, no one spoke, then the new-comer found his voice and cried, 'What the devil's going on?'

'I should have thought that was quite plain,' Lang replied evenly.

Reluctant to confront the other man, Alan turned his fury on Cassandra. 'Why in heaven's name were you letting him maul you about like that?'

'She wasn't just *letting* me,' Lang pointed out with infuriating calm, 'but actively cooperating. Though I prefer the expression ''make love to'' rather than ''maul about''.'

Pulling herself free from his restraining hands, Cassandra took a step towards Alan and began hoarsely, 'I'm sorry, I—'

'Surely all this isn't because I left without saying goodbye?' he demanded.

'No, of course it isn't.'

'Then *why*? I didn't think you even liked him.'

'I'm sorry,' she repeated, close to tears. 'I wanted to break it to you gently... I didn't want you to find out like this...'

'I bet you didn't! After the way you've always kept me at arm's length!'

As though further enraged by the thought, his face turned beetroot-red and he rushed on, 'You were so damned cool I'd started to wonder if you were frigid, when you agreed to that weekend in Paris... And still it came to nothing...

'Then, when you told me about that earlier unsavoury

incident, I must admit it made me think twice about marrying you...

'It isn't the kind of thing anyone would want their future wife to have been mixed up in... And it could well have been your own fault. I only heard one version of the story. You could have been making your own side right...

'I wondered at the time whether you'd been leading him on, asking for trouble, and now I'm—'

White to the lips, she broke in, 'I was doing no such thing! And if you felt like that why didn't you say so and ask for your ring back?'

'It would have made things difficult with you working for me. We've always been a good team and I didn't want to rock the boat, so I decided to forgive you—'

'You decided to forgive me!' She faced him with a fury equal to his own. 'For what? For something I didn't do?'

But, ignoring the interruption, he snarled, 'And this is how you repay me! With the wedding only a week away, I thought I could trust you. But you've humiliated me, made me look a complete fool...

'And I still don't know *why*, what I've ever done to deserve it... The very least I'm entitled to is an explanation... Though nothing you can say will excuse that kind of behaviour...

'When we got engaged I believed that as well as beauty and brains you had class... I thought you'd make a good wife and a marvellous hostess, be a real asset to my career... But I can see now that I made a terrible mistake. I've no intention of going through with the wedding, and I want my ring back.'

Then, disgust and loathing mingling, he said, 'No man can be expected to forgive his fiancée for acting like some trollop... If I hadn't arrived when I did you'd no doubt have ended up in bed together—'

'That's quite enough.' Lang's curt order cut through

the tirade, stopping it dead. With quiet authority he went on, 'Now you'll listen to me. I agree that you're entitled to an explanation, and I'm prepared to give you one. But first I must insist that you withdraw that remark about acting like a trollop, and apologize to Cassandra.'

Looking sullen and at a disadvantage, Alan hesitated.

His face and voice steely, Lang added, 'We both appreciate that you feel ill-used and angry, and to some extent that anger is justified. But had you known all the facts I'm quite sure you would have refrained from saying any such thing.'

Unable to stand up against the other man's cool authority, Alan muttered ungraciously, 'Very well, I apologize.'

With a brief nod, Lang continued, 'Now, these are the facts. Firstly, Cassandra is no longer your fiancée, and no longer wearing your ring. So you may certainly have it back...'

Feeling in his pocket, Lang produced the diamond cluster and tossed it to Alan, who caught it on a reflex action.

'Secondly, as Cassandra is my wife, we have every right to make love in the privacy of our own suite, and go to bed together as and when we wish.'

Watching the other man's flabbergasted face, Lang lifted Cassandra's hand to display the wedding ring. 'We were married this afternoon at San Miguel.

'I realize that, happening so suddenly, all this must have come as a shock, but I have to emphasize that Cassandra is in no way to blame. She wanted to wait and speak to you first, but I was impatient to make her my wife and I swept her off her feet, so to speak.'

'I—I don't understand,' Alan stammered. 'You've only just met.'

'Surely you've heard the rather hackneyed phrase ''love at first sight''?'

'But Cass loves...loved...' he stumbled over his tenses '...me...'

'She *thought* she did,' Lang said flatly. 'Obviously you both made a mistake, so it's just as well things have resolved themselves.' Briskly, he added, 'In view of all that's happened it might make sense to concentrate on your career for a while...'

At the word 'career' Alan made a visible effort to pull himself together, clearly wondering what effect the turn of events and his subsequent outburst had had on his future prospects.

Having made his point, with perfect timing Lang produced the sop. 'Though you are still one of the youngest departmental heads in my organization you've already proved your worth. Bearing that in mind, I've a proposition to put to you... If you intend to stay with Dalton International, that is?'

Recalling her earlier concern, Cassandra held her breath. No matter what, Alan was still an innocent party in all this and, as such, she didn't want him to lose out.

A moment later any worries that he might throw it all away were set at rest as he answered, 'W-well, yes, I—'

'Then come and have a drink at the bar, and I'll tell you what my plans are.'

Lang's manner was civil, bordering on affable as, leaving Cassandra standing cold and numb, he ushered the younger man to the door.

Since his forced apology, Alan hadn't once looked in her direction, and she had the feeling that he had already erased her from his life as easily as one might erase a printed mistake from a computer screen.

His hand on the knob, Lang turned to give her a measured glance, before closing the door quietly behind them.

She felt limp and battered, like a survivor from some disaster. Trembling in every limb, she sank on to the nearest chair and stared blindly into space while the unpleasant little scene replayed itself over and over again in her mind.

It was a while before the trembling stopped and she was able to get a grip on herself and begin to put her thoughts into some kind of order.

One thing at least was clear: Lang had been right in his assessment of the situation. Alan had felt betrayed, justifiably furious and resentful, but he'd shown no signs of being seriously hurt, and he hadn't once mentioned love.

She had fondly imagined that the Paris trip, and knowing about Sean, had strengthened their relationship, but she'd been quite wrong. His angry revelations had made that only too plain.

The fact that he'd walked in and found her in Lang's arms had obviously confirmed his earlier suspicion that she might have led Sean on.

But if he could think that, if he'd learnt so little about her true character, he'd never really known her.

He'd told her, when he'd first proposed to her, that she was just the kind of wife for an up-and-coming young executive. Though she had been pleased and flattered, all she'd needed to know was that he cared.

When he'd added, 'I love you. You're the only girl in the world for me,' she had thought herself the luckiest of women.

There was an old saying 'There's none so blind as those that will not see'. In her need for love and affection she had closed her eyes to any doubts and uncertainties, and convinced herself that he really did care. Now she knew she had been deluding herself from the first.

Discovering just how unfeeling and self-centred he could be had come as an unpleasant surprise. Yet in an odd sort of way it had also come as a relief, absolving her from some of the guilt she'd felt.

But if he hadn't walked in on them like that and been

shocked into total honesty she would have continued to...

Cassandra's train of thought came to an abrupt halt. How *had* he been able to just walk in like that? Why hadn't whoever was on the desk announced his arrival?

Her mind went back to that awful moment. She had stood paralyzed, startled out of her wits, while Lang had appeared cool and unruffled, almost as if he'd *expected* Alan to walk in on them...

She jumped as the door opened and Lang strolled in, looking, to her jaundiced eye, unbearably smug and self-satisfied.

'You'll be pleased to know that everything went smoothly,' he reported. 'Brent's on his way back to the airport without, apparently, too many regrets.

'In fact he seemed relieved to have come out of it so well. He's already started planning his new life in Switzerland and—'

Noting Cassandra's stony face, he broke off and lifted a well-marked brow. 'You don't look at all happy.'

'I'm not.'

'Decided you've sacrificed too much for him?'

Ignoring the taunt, she said, 'Alan was able to just walk in. I'd like to know how.'

'Ah... So that's what's bugging you.'

'Why didn't the desk let us know when he got here?'

In no way perturbed, Lang admitted, 'Because I asked Stephens to send him straight up.'

Her green eyes flashed. 'You knew what time he was arriving, and you started to make love to me on purpose! You *wanted* him to walk in and find me in your arms... How *could* you be so cruel?'

Standing looking down at her, his face implacable, Lang said evenly, 'There's no kind way to tell a man you've taken the woman he presumes is his. Rather than trying to spare his feelings, and be faced with endless questions or a long-drawn-out post-mortem, I decided it would easier for everyone to let him *see* how things were. One picture is worth a thousand words, or so they say.

'I wondered if he might be man enough to wade in and try to punch me on the nose. I'd have respected him a damn sight more if he had. Instead, he took it out on you. In a way I'm sorry about that. But if he'd merely been hurt and wretched you would have felt upset, riddled with guilt, despite the fact that you'd done it all for him.

'At least he showed his true colours and made you angry in your turn. In my opinion being angry is preferable to being miserable.'

'I'm glad you think so.'

'It's sad to be disillusioned,' he admitted soberly, 'but knowing the truth has to be better than being married to a man who regards you simply as a career accessory.'

Resentment and a raw hurt assaulted her equally, then almost immediately fell back to leave only a kind of dull despair.

What Lang had said was true. But, having lived through a loveless childhood, she wanted, *needed* warmth and affection, and it was bitter to think that for the sake of one man who didn't love her she had married another man who didn't love her.

Lifting her chin, she met his eyes and asked trenchantly, 'And what do *you* regard me as?'

Just for a moment he looked ruffled, disconcerted. Then he queried, 'What do you think?'

'I think I'm nothing but a temporary whim.'

Lang's jaw tightened. 'Oh, a little more than that. At the very least an obsession.'

An *obsession*... The word hung on the air. Believing him, Cassandra shuddered.

What was it about her? she wondered bleakly. For the second time in her life, she had become the innocent victim of a man's obsession.

Though perhaps in Sean's case not *entirely* innocent. It was true she had never led him on, at least not intentionally, but she should have seen where such obsessiveness was leading and broken things off before it got out of hand.

Penny had tried to warn her, but she hadn't fully appreciated the danger, and had been loath to take the kind of drastic action her friend had advocated.

By the time she had admitted that *something* would have to be done, it had been too late.

She shivered again. The memories were like a bruise on her soul.

Seeing that betraying movement and her loss of colour, Lang said, 'But that's enough soul-searching. Let's unwind with a glass of champagne and some music.'

A moment later the room was filled with the haunting strains of an old Jerome Kern melody.

Having eased out the champagne cork and poured the still smoking wine, Lang handed her a glass, and sat down beside her.

She had a sudden vivid memory of Sean turning up on her doorstep that awful night with a bottle of champagne...

Lang's arm slid around her shoulders, breaking into her thoughts. Still half trapped in the past, she froze. Feeling her stiffen, he asked lightly, 'Still angry?' His hand moved to caress the line of her jaw. 'Let's forget everything but—'

Jumping up, she dropped the champagne glass, which spilt its contents and rolled across the carpet. 'Leave me alone!'

He rose to his feet and, picking up her glass, put that and his own on the coffee table, before saying flatly, 'In case it's slipped your mind, we were married today, and this is our wedding night.'

Every nerve in her body tightening in alarm, she

backed away, her hands flung out to ward him off. 'I don't want to sleep with you.'

'I could understand this show of reluctance if you hadn't slept with me before. But last night you were more than willing.'

Through stiff lips she said, 'Last night was different.'

'Why? I'm just the same man, except that now I'm your husband.'

She shook her head in mute rejection.

Softly, dangerously, he pointed out, 'You agreed to be my wife.'

'I was blackmailed into it.'

'You could have told me to go to hell... Almost any other woman would have.'

'I—I couldn't leave Alan to face—'

Lang laughed harshly. 'Did you really believe I'd ruin Brent? *Did you*, Cassandra?'

Wanting to say yes, she hesitated, unable to. She had told herself she couldn't risk it, but had she ever truly believed he would go to those lengths?

His dark blue eyes intent, Lang pursued, 'Wasn't it that, after last night, you'd realized Brent wasn't the man for you, and you *wanted* to marry me?'

Had she at some strange, subconscious level wanted to marry him? She had fooled herself into believing that Alan loved her. Had she also fooled herself into believing that this was a forced marriage?

Possibly, because she knew he'd loved his wife and he didn't love her, she'd needed an excuse for what the sane side of her would have regarded as utter madness...

'No, it certainly wasn't.' To hide her sudden doubts she made her denial more emphatic.

With a sigh of exasperation, Lang said curtly, 'Well, even if I'm wrong, I'm keeping my part of the bargain and I expect you to keep yours.'

Looking into a face that held no sign of tenderness or

compassion, she saw another man's ruthless face mirrored there.

Panic took a fresh hold. 'No, I can't go through with it. I don't want you to touch me.'

'You didn't feel like that earlier.'

Lifting her chin, she cried defiantly, 'Well, I do now!'

A white line appeared around his mouth. 'Before Brent turned up I could have taken you to bed and made love to you, and you'd have responded whole-heartedly. If this sudden rejection is just to get back at me, it won't work.'

For an instant she thought of trying to explain, but he was obviously in no mood to listen to reason.

'I've no intention of letting you play hard to get. I want you in my bed and I want the marriage consummated...'

Lang Dalton didn't care about her feelings as a woman. He was just like Sean. The old nightmare had come alive again.

She began to shiver violently, the defiant façade cracked wide open.

His eyes narrowing on her paper-white face, Lang said abruptly, 'For God's sake don't look like that!'

'Please don't force me,' she begged. 'I couldn't bear it...'

Sounding shocked, he said, 'Much as I want you, I have absolutely no intention of trying to force you...'

She looked once again into his tough face and saw stark need etched in every line, but this time she also saw the discipline and self-control that governed that need and knew she was safe.

He wasn't like Sean. Out of remembered fear, she had seriously misjudged him.

'What kind of a brute do you think I am?' His jaw was set and angry. 'I've never tried to force a woman in my life, and I don't intend to start now.'

'I—I'm sorry.' Miserably, she added, 'I don't know you very well.'

'No, you don't.'

Her heart like lead, she stood silent and motionless while, his fingers still lightly gripping her upper arms, he looked down at her.

Earlier in the evening they had been easy together, sharing a joke, enjoying each other's company. Now she was taut and wretched, and he was furious. They were on opposite sides of an abyss that it seemed neither could bridge.

So where did they go from here? Where *was* there to go?

Apparently wondering the same thing, Lang frowned.

A moment later, as though he'd made up his mind, the anger was wiped from his face and he said, 'Well, even if you don't want to sleep with me, this is no way to spend our wedding night.'

Soft, romantic music was still playing quietly in the background, and, putting an arm around her waist, he suggested, 'Let's dance.'

She was tall for a woman, slender and supple. He was wide-shouldered, slim-hipped and well-muscled, with an athlete's grace of movement.

They fitted together like two halves of a whole.

Cassandra gave a little sigh, her feeling of depression lifting. Though they had never danced with each other before, he was strangely familiar, easy to follow, as though they were attuned to one another's steps. Without stopping to analyse why, she found it pleasant, oddly comforting, to be in his arms.

After a while he drew her closer and put his cheek against her hair.

The residue of misery draining away, she closed her eyes and let her head rest on his shoulder. She could feel the warmth of his flesh through the thin silk of his shirt, smell his faintly spicy aftershave and the clean, slightly salty scent of his skin.

The previous night, though ardent and receptive, a certain shyness, perhaps due to lack of experience, had made her hesitate to touch him.

Now she found herself wanting to both touch and taste his skin, to follow the smooth ripple of muscle with her tongue, to feel the light sprinkling of body hair crisp beneath her fingertips...

As though he knew exactly what she was thinking and feeling, his lips brushed her hair, and his hand began to travel lightly over her body, tracing the line of her spine, the curve of her hip, the shape of her buttocks.

His touch was electric, and she pictured him fondling her breasts, smoothing over the sensitive skin of her stomach, making love to her...

Unexpected and unbidden, desire stirred into life and began to heat her blood and send her pulses leaping.

When they came to a halt by his bedroom door, she lifted her head and they stood together, face to face, hip to hip.

Pressing her gently back against the panels, he leaned into her, his body hard against her softness, and lightly circled his pelvis.

She gasped and looked up at him with wide, dazed eyes. Perhaps he mistook that dazed look for indecision, because he murmured softly, reassuringly, 'Don't worry, we'll take it slowly. I won't do anything you don't want me to do.'

When she said nothing, he coaxed, 'Shall we begin with a kiss and see where it leads?'

Knowing quite well where it was going to lead, she stood on tiptoe and kissed his lips.

Mouths clinging closely, stroking and caressing, they began to undress each other, he with deft efficiency, she, having no previous practice and more to take off, with somewhat less.

Shirt buttons were simple, the knotted tie not so easy, and when her untutored fingers struggled for what seemed an age to unfasten the clip at the waist of his trousers he was forced to help her.

When they were both naked he carried her into the bedroom and, throwing back the covers, laid her on the king-sized bed.

With a little inarticulate murmur, she wound her arms around his neck and tried to pull him down to her, as eager a bride as any bridegroom could have wished for.

But, unwinding her arms, he stretched out beside her and began to make love to her with unhurried skill, touching and tasting, sensual and erotic, making full use of every erogenous zone.

Within seconds she was feeling everything he wanted her to feel, while he went on exploring, probing, arousing...

His hands and mouth were pleasuring her when a light flick of his tongue made her jerk and brought a gasp to her throat. 'Do you like that?' he asked softly.

'Yes,' she breathed.

'Shall I go on?'

'Oh, yes...'

'Then lie still; don't thrash about like that.'

He was a master of his art, in total command of her mind and body. Wringing the most exquisite sensations from her, he kept her on the brink until she thought she could stand no more.

Only when soft whimpering sounds were rising in her throat, wordless little pleas, did he give her the satisfaction she craved, leaving her quivering and emotionally exhausted.

Turning away from her, he pulled a silk sheet over them to combat the coolness of the air-conditioning, and suggested flatly, 'Time to get some rest, don't you think?'

The euphoria abruptly faded and died. Last night she

had gone to sleep in his arms. Now, lying with a good eighteen inches of space between them, she experienced a sharp sense of disappointment. Of loss.

This wasn't the kind of wedding night she had envisaged, and though he had given her the most intense physical pleasure, she felt in some obscure way cheated.

It had been just sexual gratification, and that on its own, with nothing deeper, was a poor substitute for what they had shared the previous night.

Yes, that was it, *shared*.

Perhaps it was the sharing that made all the difference. The *mutual* pleasure. Pleasure given and received. She had given nothing. But then he'd asked for nothing.

Knowing he too was fully aroused, she had expected him to go on and find his own satisfaction. But, exerting the most incredible control, this man who was her husband, a man with rights, had stayed purposely aloof and distant.

Why had he deliberately held back? she wondered dismally. Was it to make a point? To prove his absolute mastery? Or because, beneath that calm exterior, he was still furious?

A kind of inner certainty insisted it was almost certainly the latter.

But as she didn't love him, did it matter?

Yes, it did. She didn't want him to be angry with her, to be cold and distant. She wanted back the man who had smiled and teased her, who had been warm and passionate, who had last night held her close and settled her head on his shoulder.

Well, in that case, it was up to her to make the first move. If she could whip up the necessary courage...

The curtains hadn't been drawn, and the glow from the plethora of neon that lit up Las Vegas at night made the room quite light. Turning her head, Cassandra looked at the man by her side.

Lang was stretched on his back, the sheet pulled up

to his waist. His heavy-lidded eyes were closed, the long, gold-tipped lashes lying like fans on his hard cheeks.

His breathing was shallow and even, and he appeared to be asleep, but something about his very stillness convinced her he wasn't.

For a while, fearing rejection, she lay where she was and watched him. Then, taking her courage in both hands, she moved across the eighteen inches or so of no man's land and snuggled up against him.

When he continued to lie silent and unmoving, she let her hand rove over his chest, touching and exploring as she'd wanted to earlier. Finding the warm hollow at the base of his throat, following the clean line of his collarbone, learning the leathery texture of his small flat nipples...

His hand suddenly closing over hers made her gasp. 'You'd better understand straight away that I'm not made of stone. Unless you're prepared to take the consequences, it would be sensible to get back on your own side of the bed and leave plenty of space between us.'

'That's no way to spend our wedding night.' Purposely she echoed his earlier sentiments, adding spiritedly, 'I'd much sooner stay where I am.'

'What's the matter? Did I fail to satisfy you?'

'I certainly didn't get what I wanted,' she answered obliquely.

'Oh? What did you want?'

She chose her words carefully. 'I wanted to make love with you.'

An edge to his voice, he said, 'I certainly didn't get that impression previously. You were anything but willing.'

'I'm willing now.'

'Look, you don't have to make any gestures. The last thing I want is a wife driven to submit by either a sense of duty or an uneasy conscience. I want what I had last night, an equal partner, someone who isn't just willing, but warm and eager, and responsive.

'Bearing that in mind I'm prepared to wait until you want me as much as I want you...'

'But I do want you.'

Still he made no move, and, her nerve rapidly running out, in a last desperate gamble she pushed herself up on one elbow and touched her lips to his in a series of soft, baby kisses.

'You're playing with fire, Cassandra,' he warned.

'I thought a little warmth wouldn't go amiss.' She took his lower lip between her teeth and bit it delicately.

Reacting at last to the deliberate provocation, he muttered something that could have been an oath, and rolled, pinning her beneath him.

Until the previous night she'd had no real idea how voluptuous, how erotic and exciting it was, to feel skin against skin, naked flesh against naked flesh. Now, the moment he touched her, her body flashed to full arousal and welcomed his.

This time there was no slow and careful build-up. Instead of being gentle and considerate, his lovemaking was fierce and demanding, taking everything she had to give, spinning her entire being until her mind was dizzy and her soul had lost its way.

When it was over she lay quietly, cradling his head to her breast, while slow tears trickled down her cheeks.

She had never known anything like this feeling of complete union, of being swept up and made whole by another human being. It was wonderful, terrifying, awe-inspiring.

But Lang must have. In fact even more so. He'd loved his wife, and love would add the extra spiritual dimension.

If only he'd loved *her*.

She knew with utter certainty that she could have loved him. He was tough, manipulative and autocratic, but he was also caring, compassionate and sensitive. A bitter-sweet mixture.

Alan's nature had been basically cold, whereas Lang's, beneath the veneer of cool composure he habitually wore, was an ardent one.

Their marriage would never lack the fiery heat of passion. If only it also had the gentle warmth of love. A shared love would have made the experience perfect...

Lang stirred and lifted his head. His eyes still held a slightly dazed look, and a fine sheen of perspiration dewed his forehead and upper lip.

A second or so later the dazed look vanished and the dark blue eyes sharpened into focus. 'Did I hurt you?' he asked abruptly.

'No,' Cassandra said.

'Then why are you crying?'

'I—I didn't know I was.'

'Are you sure I didn't hurt you?'

She saw by his face that he was disturbed by her tears. More positively, she said, 'Quite sure.'

His weight lifted from her, but instead of turning away he gathered her up and held her close. One hand moving up and down her spine in an age-old gesture of comfort and reassurance, he said, 'I'm sorry if I was rough with you. I shouldn't have treated you that way just because I was angry. But when you froze up earlier it came as a shock...'

Perhaps this was the time to try and explain what had made her freeze.

But would he, like Alan, believe that she had led Sean on? The possibility made her hesitate and kept the words unspoken.

A moment later the chance was gone, as Lang went on, 'I believe any woman should have the right to say no, if that's how she genuinely feels. But it's another matter entirely when she intentionally blows hot and cold, either to assert her power, or to try and make a fool of a man.'

Shocked, Cassandra protested, 'I never meant to blow hot and cold.'

'Perhaps not,' he admitted bleakly. 'But that's how it seemed, and being treated in that way brought back too many bad memories...'

He didn't seem to have much luck with the women in his life, Cassandra thought sadly. His mother had sacrificed him, one of his previous lovers had clearly made him embittered, he'd lost both a beloved sister and his first wife, and now he had a wife he'd had to coerce into marrying him. A woman he might want, but one he neither cared for nor trusted.

'Lang, I...'

He put a finger to her lips, stopping the words. 'We won't talk about it any more.' Pillowing her head at the comfortable junction between his chest and shoulder, he said, 'Go to sleep now, and don't worry; I won't touch you again.'

This was only the second time in her life that she hadn't slept alone. Sharing a bed with someone else was a new experience and one that—rather to her surprise, never having thought of herself as a physical person—she found enjoyable.

She could feel the steady beat of his heart and the touch of his breath as it stirred her hair; she was conscious of the rise and fall of his chest, the strength of his arm holding her close, and the length of one hair-roughened leg against the smoothness of her own.

This time she was ready to sleep, but it was a while before her mind, not so at ease as her body, would relax its grip on consciousness and allow oblivion to come.

CHAPTER EIGHT

CASSANDRA drifted up to the surface slowly from a dream of pure joy. Still half asleep, she lay with her eyes closed, savouring the bliss.

Lang had been making love to her. He had stroked and undressed her, and while she had lain breathless beneath the soft rain of his kisses he had murmured over and over again how much he loved her and how much he needed her to love him.

Her heart full to overflowing, she had kissed him back and told him she did; that it had been love at first sight. A love she had waited all her life to both give and receive...

Now, waking to a new day, she realized that it had only been a foolish dream, born of longing and need. Yet it had been seductive, full of sweetness and pleasure and comfort.

Sighing, she opened her eyes. It was quite late, she judged; thousand-watt sunshine filtered through the curtains, making the attractive room bright.

Momentarily dazzled, she blinked, and looked up to see Lang, propped on one elbow, gazing down at her. His dark blond hair was rumpled and his jaw rough with stubble. His blue eyes held a look of bleak unhappiness that made her catch her breath.

The memory of her dream still clinging like golden cobwebs, she held out her arms to him, her face unconsciously tender.

The bleakness faded, to be replaced by a look she couldn't decipher. 'Sure you've got the right man?'

'What?'

'You weren't mistaking me for Brent?'

'No, I wasn't.' Feeling rebuffed, she let her arms drop to her sides.

His face grim, he harked back. 'Last night, you said I hadn't hurt you.'

'You hadn't.'

'Then tell me why you were crying.'

Taken by surprise, she spoke the exact truth. 'I was just thinking of how it might have been.'

The strong jaw tightened, and she knew he'd misunderstood. He had assumed she'd been comparing their wedding night with the one she might have shared with Alan.

Before she could make any attempt to correct that assumption, Lang turned away and, pushing himself into a sitting position, said harshly, 'No wonder you were dreaming about him... Dreaming *he* was your bridegroom.'

Struggling up, she sat back against the pillows, her cloud of ash-brown hair tumbled about her shoulders. Pulling up the sheet to cover her nakedness, she denied, 'I wasn't dreaming anything of the kind.'

'But if you could wave a magic wand and have him here beside you, instead of me, you would?'

'No,' she said flatly. And knew it was the truth.

Seeing Lang looked unconvinced, she added, 'As far as I'm concerned Alan belongs in a past that's over and done with.'

Both her past and her carefully planned future had been overturned and devastated. It was much too late to save either. The only thing possible now was to try to regain her equilibrium, and find, if she could, some kind of future stability.

As though he had the ability to walk in and out of her mind, Lang queried, 'So you feel able to look forward to our future together? To a marriage made in heaven?'

Nettled by that hateful mockery, she lashed out, 'What

a delightfully old-fashioned phrase. I wasn't aware people used it any longer.'

He hadn't expected her to hit back, and just for an instant the merest flicker of his eyelids betrayed his surprise. Then, with a taunting smile, he queried, 'But perhaps you don't believe there is such a thing as a marriage made in heaven?'

'I don't know,' she admitted.

'So you weren't anticipating one with Brent?'

Stung afresh, she said sharply, 'Would you regard your first marriage as heaven-made?'

As soon as the words left her lips, she regretted her ill-judged retaliation. The last thing she wanted to do was stir up unhappy memories.

Seeing his face stiffen, she begged hurriedly, 'I'm sorry; please forget I said that.'

After a moment the tautness relaxed, and he pursued, 'What about *our* marriage?'

'If there is such a thing as a marriage made in heaven surely it would be, as the name implies, something rare and precious? A gift only given to the lucky few who really belong together?'

Studying her face, he pursed his lips. 'So you don't think ours will turn out to be one of them?'

Wondering why he seemed to be deliberately tormenting her, she asked flatly, 'Do you?'

'It has the potential to be.'

'Really?' She made no attempt to hide her derision 'How can you tell?'

His eyes glinted. 'Guess.'

Sarcastically, she suggested, 'It must be because we got off to such a good start?'

'Full marks.'

'I'm afraid you've lost me somewhere.'

'The first night we spent together was wonderful... Now tell me it was merely sex.'

A tinge of pink appearing along her high cheekbones, she said, 'I was about to.'

'But good sex is the key. Get that right and everything else falls into place. If the physical side doesn't work, nothing does.'

'There are more important things than sex in a marriage.'

'Such as?'

'Respect, honesty, kindness, caring...'

'They may be *as* important, not *more* important. And if you had married Brent how many of those would have been present?'

Why did he keep dragging Alan into it? she wondered vexedly.

Watching her face, one eyebrow slightly raised, he waited. Soft mouth set, she refused to answer.

With a little shrug, he went on, 'And even *with* all those things, if the vital spark is missing it won't work. Marriage should be based on passion, not reason or practicalities.'

When she remained silent, his face sardonic, he suggested, 'But as our true forte is non-verbal communication, suppose I give you a practical demonstration of just what I mean?'

Cassandra bit her lip. This wasn't how she'd wanted it to be. She had hoped they could find some common ground and become friends, or at the very least non-combatants.

But since the previous night his mood had changed. Then he'd been willing to comfort her, now he seemed bent on punishing her.

For what? Because he believed she'd been thinking of Alan while he'd been making love to her?

If Lang had cared anything for her, she might have wondered if he was jealous, but, convinced that all he felt was possessive, she guessed it was simply masculine pique.

He curved a hand around her cheek, his thumb moving caressingly. 'As you've denied it was Brent you were dreaming of, perhaps you'd like to start the ball rolling by giving me a kiss?'

Pulling back, her voice carefully polite, she said, 'No, I wouldn't, thank you. I'd like to go to the bathroom.'

She got out of bed and, very aware that he was watching, pulled on the thin cotton robe she'd brought with her. Endeavouring to appear cool and unhurried, she headed for the bathroom on legs that trembled, and closed the door behind her.

For a second her hand hovered over the bolt, but somehow she resisted the temptation. He would almost certainly hear it being pushed home, and she didn't want to give him the satisfaction of knowing how much he'd managed to rattle her.

In any case what would be the use? It would only be a temporary reprieve. A matter of time before she was forced to face him again. She could hardly spend the day locked in the bathroom.

Her toilet bag had been placed on one of the luxurious vanity units and, having brushed her teeth, she pinned up her hair ready for the shower.

The water was good and hot, just how she liked it, and normally she would have been tempted to linger under it. But, very aware of that unbolted door, she showered as quickly as possible, and without her usual enjoyment.

Still wreathed in clouds of perfumed steam, she turned off the jet, slid open the frosted-glass panel and, soap in her eyes, was fumbling blindly for the towel, when she heard the bathroom door open and close again.

'Having problems?' Lang's deep voice held a touch of amusement.

Naked and vulnerable, her eyes smarting, she said, 'None that a towel wouldn't solve.'

'Then allow me.' A moment later a towel was placed in her hand.

Hastily she rubbed her eyes and blinked a few times. When she was able to see again, she found his tall, muscular figure was completely blocking the entrance to the shower stall. He hadn't a stitch on.

Reading her expression, he asked trenchantly, 'Wishing you'd bolted the door after all?'

'I don't know what you mean.'

'Oh, come on! You ran like a frightened rabbit.'

'I did no such thing,' she denied indignantly.

He took the towel from her nerveless fingers and tossed it aside. 'Then you're not scared?'

She lifted her chin. 'Certainly not. Why should I be scared?'

'Because seeing you standing there, naked and wet and gleaming like Aphrodite, is giving me even more ideas.'

'I won't let it worry me,' she assured him mendaciously.

He raised a mocking brow. 'My, you *have* got brave all of a sudden. How come?'

Her throat tight, she swallowed to relieve the tension. 'You've already proved how good you are at self-control.'

'You can't expect a newly married man to exercise too much of that.'

'You said you wanted me to be...' About to say 'willing', she substituted, 'Eager.'

Stepping in beside her, and sliding the panel closed, he smiled. 'And you're not?'

His eyes were on her breasts, and in response to that look she felt her nipples firm betrayingly.

'No.' Once more she was forced to swallow hard.

He reached out and drew her against the length of his body. Matching contour to contour. Hard male muscle against yielding female flesh.

'You said—' She broke off with a gasp as, bending his head, he nuzzled his face against her breasts, the sandpaper rasp of his bristles against the sensitive peaks almost unbearably erotic.

'What did I say?' He circled a damp pink nipple with his tongue.

Distractedly, she whispered, 'I can't remember…'

Shaken between passion and laughter, he assured her softly, 'I never said I wouldn't try to change your mind… Have you ever shared a shower?'

Her throat dry, she croaked, 'No. I've led a very sheltered life.'

'Then I think you should make up for it by having an exciting honeymoon. Starting now…'

It was an hour or more before, showered and dressed, they finally emerged on to the terrace. After the relative coolness of the air-conditioned suite, it was like walking into an oven.

Brassy sunshine poured down from a deep blue sky and the heat hung motionless, golden and sticky as melted honey.

'We can eat inside if you like?' Lang suggested.

The remembrance of what had gone before making her feel shy, Cassandra answered without looking at him, 'I'd much rather be outside, if that suits you?'

'Yes, I've always preferred to eat alfresco.'

Leading her over to the vine-shaded table, where a buffet-style lunch was waiting, Lang pulled out her chair and helped her to seafood and salad, before sitting down opposite.

Several fans placed in strategic positions wafted cooler air and made what would have been a desiccating temperature pleasant.

'Not too hot?' he queried.

'No, it's wonderful. I've always loved heat and sunshine.'

'Nina couldn't stand the sun,' he said abruptly, 'and she disliked too much heat. That was one of the reasons she preferred San Francisco. It tends to be cooler further north.'

Feeling as if she'd been slapped, Cassandra picked up her knife and fork. Only a short time ago Lang had been making passionate love to her, but already he was thinking of his first wife.

Was he still missing her? Had he been comparing the two of them? Finding *her* sadly wanting?

Alan's description ran through her mind. 'He married a woman the media once described as ''America's most beautiful socialite''. I gather she comes from one of California's top families, the kind who hobnob with film stars and presidents.'

Cassandra was pierced by a sharp pang of envy, not for Nina's position or beauty, but simply because Lang had loved her.

Instantly she felt ashamed. She couldn't possibly be jealous of a dead woman. It was almost obscene. And, as she'd reminded herself earlier, to be truly jealous one had to *love*, and despite her dream all she felt for Lang was a strong physical attraction.

She certainly didn't love him. How could she? Yet the thought that she might be having his child no longer scared her half to death. If she was, it would create a bond between them...

Busy with her thoughts, she pushed her food around her plate, her eating a mere pretence, until Lang broke the silence to remark, 'I thought we'd stay in these parts for our honeymoon, unless there's anywhere else you'd particularly like to go?'

'Honeymoon?' she echoed.

'You sound surprised. Weren't you expecting a honeymoon?'

'No.' In truth, things had happened so fast she had never given it a thought.

'Hadn't you and Brent planned a honeymoon...?'

There it was again, she thought with a sigh, like probing a sore tooth.

'Weren't you going somewhere wildly romantic?'

Ignoring the taunt, she said flatly, 'Because the wedding date had been brought forward, we'd decided to do without a honeymoon.'

In fact the decision had been unilateral. Though not short of money, Alan, who had a careful streak, had insisted that they spend what they could afford on refurbishing his parents' house rather than 'squandering it on something we don't need.'

'No honeymoon?' Lang tutted. 'Well, with a change of bridegroom, you get a change of plan,' he told her, the mockery evident.

She squared up to him. 'I'm surprised that a man who's so busy making money can find time for a honeymoon.'

Unruffled, he said, 'I find time for anything I want to do. Any man in my position who doesn't can be called a fool.'

'Well, I might call you a lot of things,' she muttered, 'but that wouldn't be one of them.'

'You intrigue me.' His gaze caught and held hers. 'What would you call me?'

His eyes were very dark blue with darker rings to the irises and, radiating from the pupil, like sunshine trapped in the depths of water, tiny rays of gold.

Looking into those eyes made her strangely dizzy.

Somehow she tore her gaze away and answered, 'Cool, determined, ruthless, arrogant...'

But he was also warm, generous, and human. A tough man who, at times, seemed oddly vulnerable.

'Hardly a catalogue of virtues,' he remarked dryly. 'Anyone might think you hated me.'

'Anyone might be right.'

'Married to a man you think you hate,' he murmured musingly.

'I don't *think*, I'm sure.'

'Well, I'll have to see what I can do to change your mind. That should make for an interesting honeymoon.' Then, like a rattlesnake striking, he said, 'And it might be better than being married to a man you thought you loved.'

Why did she take him on? she wondered bitterly. In a battle of words, with a quicker brain and a sharper wit, he always emerged the clear winner.

Throwing in the towel, she said, 'This honeymoon you keep mentioning... How long were you thinking of?'

He poured coffee for them both before answering, 'A month.'

'A *month*?' She'd expected him to say a few days. A week at the most.

'You sound less than thrilled at the prospect.'

'There's a problem.'

'Oh?'

About to say she'd left her trousseau at home, she changed it to, 'I've hardly any clothes.'

'I don't see that as a problem.' A smile tugging at his lips, he added, 'As a matter of fact I much prefer you without clothes... And as I personally regard the ideal honeymoon destination as bed—'

'We can't spend a month in bed,' she broke in, her face growing hot.

'Oh, I don't know... But just in case we do want to venture out a spot of shopping might not be a bad idea... In point of fact,' he added slyly, 'I'd made it the second thing on the afternoon's agenda.'

Afraid to ask what the first one was, she remained silent.

Apparently reading her thoughts, and hell-bent on tormenting her, he said, 'Just at the moment I'm a bit bushed, but in a little while if you'd like to…' Leaning forward, he whispered a suggestion in her ear that deepened her flush to scarlet.

Her pulses leapt wildly and, putting her cup down with a clatter, she said huskily, 'No, I wouldn't!'

'Ah, well,' he sighed theatrically, 'it's early days yet.'

For a moment or two he studied her burning face, then, taking pity on her, changed the subject to say briskly, 'Yesterday you mentioned a flatmate… Penny…? Won't she be expecting you back sometime tomorrow morning?'

'Yes…'

'In that case it might be a good idea to give her a call and put her in the picture.'

'Yes, I—I really ought to,' Cassandra agreed weakly, wondering how on earth she was going to put Penny in the picture without the other girl thinking she'd gone stark, staring mad.

'Let's see.' Lang consulted his watch. 'Allowing for the time difference it should be about nine-thirty p.m. in London. Is she likely to be home?'

'Yes.'

He rose. 'Then better get it over with.' Taking both her hands, he pulled her to her feet and followed her back into the penthouse.

Picturing Penny's surprise and sheer incredulity when she told her the news, Cassandra reached for the phone.

'Mind if I listen in?' Lang queried blandly.

Though she had no intention of telling Penny the whole story, she would have preferred a private conversation. But, feeling unable to say so, her voice dry, she agreed, 'Be my guest,' and tapped in the number.

Lang flicked on the microphone button and, sitting down, pulled Cassandra onto his lap, holding her there when she would have wriggled free.

After a few second's delay, Penny answered, and,

sounding surprised, said, 'Cass? I thought you'd be on the plane by now.'

'Well, I would have been, only everything's changed...'

'So where are you? Still in San Francisco, I presume?'

Very conscious of the muscular thighs beneath her buttocks and the firm stomach her hip was resting against, Cassandra broke out in a hot sweat. 'No, I'm in Las Vegas,' she managed.

'Las Vegas? What on earth are you doing in Las Vegas?' Before Cassandra could answer, Penny gave a sudden squeal. 'Don't tell me you've gone and got married?'

'Well, yes, but—'

'Good for you! I didn't know Alan had it in him. Of course I'm disappointed not to have been there but I don't—'

'It isn't Alan I've married,' Cassandra broke in desperately.

There was dead silence. Then, 'Say that again.'

'It isn't Alan I've married.'

Sounding as though she thought the whole thing was some kind of joke, Penny asked, 'So who *is* the lucky man?'

'Lang Dalton.'

'Pull the other one, it's got bells on it.'

'I'm not kidding.'

'Crikey! Then tell me all.' Now she sounded breathless with excitement.

'It's a long story and not easy to explain over the phone—' the fact that Lang was kissing his way down the side of her neck and shoulder was making it even harder '—but I changed my mind about marrying Alan.'

'I've no quibble about that. It may be the most sensible thing you ever did...' Penny had never tried to hide her lack of enthusiasm for Cassandra's choice of future husband. 'So long as you haven't jumped out of the frying-pan into the fire... So what's happening?'

'Alan's got his ring back and he should be on his way home...'

'And you're in Las Vegas with Lang Dalton?'

'Yes.'

'He must be a fast worker! Just a minute, we are talking about *the* Lang Dalton?'

'Yes.'

'I've always wanted to have a friend who's married to a millionaire... But seriously, Cass, I hope you'll be very happy.'

'Thank you... I'm afraid it will mean you having to get a new flatmate...' Cassandra's voice wobbled dangerously. For the first time it was really sinking in that she wasn't going back to London, that *that* chapter of her life had ended.

'I might see if I can manage the rent without. I don't fancy sharing with just anyone...

'But before I burst with curiosity, tell me how you came to be Mrs Dalton...' Then she said sharply, 'Wait a minute; didn't I once hear he was married...?'

Wits scattered, Cassandra was wondering what to say, when Penny added, 'I just hope he isn't trying to take you for a ride...'

Removing the receiver from Cassandra's unsteady fingers, Lang said smoothly, 'Hello, Miss Lane... Lang Dalton speaking...'

There was an audible gulp from the other end.

'I feel I should assure you that Cassandra and I really are married, and that everything is above board.'

Clearly embarrassed because she hadn't realized he was listening, Penny said, 'I'm sorry, Mr Dalton, but I'm fond of Cass and I—'

'There's no need to apologize,' he assured her pleasantly. 'I appreciate your concern for your friend. As you rightly said, I have been married previously, but my first wife died some six months ago, so when I met Cassandra—'

Breaking off, he queried, 'Tell me, Miss Lane, do you believe in love at first sight?'

'It's the only sort I do believe in,' Penny answered, sounding herself again, 'apart from the more placid kinds of affection, that is. But if you see someone and you think *Wow!* that kind of chemistry is usually right.'

'A woman after my own heart,' Lang congratulated her. With no change of tone, he added, 'I understand you were expecting to be Cassandra's bridesmaid?'

'Yes, I was.' Momentarily Penny sounded wistful. 'But I'm delighted things have turned out this way. It's just like a fairy tale.'

'Well, to make up for any slight disappointment, why don't you come for a visit? Say in about a month's time.'

'You mean come over to the States?'

'Don't you fancy a trip to California?'

'I certainly do!' Penny began eagerly. Then, coming down to earth with a bump, she said, 'But I've already had a holiday this year, so I doubt if I could manage the time off work or—' About to say 'or the air fare', she bit off the words.

'Well, as you work for me, taking time off will be no problem, so if you're in agreement I'll make arrangements for you to fly on the company jet.'

'Marvellous!'

'Then we'll expect to see you when we get back from our honeymoon... Unless you'd like to come a few days early and see something of Vegas?'

'Oooh... It's always been one of my dreams to see Las Vegas... But I really can't butt in when you're on your honeymoon.'

'If we thought you'd be butting in, we wouldn't be inviting you.'

'Well, I—'

'Then we'll regard it as settled. I'll be in touch again nearer the time.'

'Thank you.' Penny sounded as if she was floating on cloud nine.

'Now I'll pass you back to Cassandra for a *private* talk. But don't keep her too long; we have a full afternoon's schedule, hopefully starting with—'

Pink-cheeked, Cassandra fairly snatched the phone out of his hand, and made to rise.

Laughing, he let her go, and, switching off the microphone, headed for the door.

'Okay?' Penny queried.

'Yes, he's gone.'

'Is he as sexy as he sounds?'

'And the rest.'

'So that chemistry was there from the first?'

'You could say that.'

'How did Alan take it? My guess would be wounded pride rather than a broken heart.'

'Your guess isn't far wrong.'

'So when did you actually get married?'

'Yesterday afternoon.'

'Cass, can I ask you something?'

'Of course.'

'Is everything going all right...? I mean, after what happened in Paris... You didn't...?'

'Freeze up, you mean? Anything but.'

'Thank God!' Penny said fervently. 'I'd begun to think that swine had screwed you up totally...'

The girls chatted for a while longer, then Penny said, 'I'd better go. Your lord and master said not to keep you too long, and though he sounds a lot like Mr Wonderful personified I should imagine he can be quite formidable if he's crossed...

'Well, see you in about a month's time, and thank you both. I can hardly believe it! In the meantime send me a card from Las Vegas…if you can manage to write postcards in bed, that is.'

Cassandra replaced the receiver and stood staring into space. Penny had said 'thank you *both*'… But, though delighted, *she'd* had nothing to do with the invitation. It had been Lang's idea, and she was beginning to know him well enough to be certain that he never did anything without a good reason.

So why had he invited Penny over? What was his motive?

'All set?' Lang's voice broke into her thoughts.

Looking up, she saw that, tall and wide-shouldered, he was lounging in the doorway.

'Something wrong?' he queried. 'You seem a bit pensive.'

She turned to face him. 'Why did you ask Penny to come over?'

He lifted a brow with that quizzical look she was starting to know well. 'Don't you want her to come? I thought you'd be pleased.'

'Of course I want her to come, and I am pleased. I just wondered *why*.'

'Call it an impulse.'

'I wouldn't have put you down as the impulsive kind.'

'Ah, but there's still a lot you don't know about me…'

Cassandra sighed. He was an expert at stonewalling, and it seemed clear that he had no intention of telling her.

'At the moment,' he went on, 'I have an impulse to take you in my arms and kiss you. But if I did we'd end up going back to bed, and as you vetoed that idea earlier… Unless you've changed your mind?'

'No, I haven't.'

'Then shopping it is.'

'It won't take too long,' she said almost apologetically. 'I just need a few things to tide me over, and I can't afford to spend too much—'

His voice sharp, he broke in, 'Surely it's a husband's prerogative to buy his wife's clothes…?'

The fact that he was her husband was so new to her that she tended to forget.

'And as I'm interested in how you look I'd like a say in choosing them.'

'I wasn't sure whether you'd want to come,' she said uncertainly. 'A lot of men can't abide shopping.'

'I don't happen to be one of them. So let's go and get your trousseau.'

He escorted her downstairs and across the lobby to the shopping mall, with its rich and glittering parade of shops and boutiques.

Most of the top fashion names were there, and the clothes were a dream. Instead of having to ask the price and spend with care, she was free to select whatever she wanted, and she found herself enjoying the novel experience.

But her main pleasure stemmed from the fact that Lang was interested. It made it all so much more fun. He had very definite ideas on how he wanted her to look, but happily their tastes coincided and most of the things she chose were simple and elegant.

They began with exquisite, cobwebby undies and glamorous nightwear, most of which Lang selected, before going on to buy day and evening clothes.

Because her wardrobe was small and tended to be mix-and-match, Cassandra usually chose neutral shades and, apart from black and white, avoided stronger colours.

Amongst the things Lang gave his approval to were khaki linen trousers, a beige-coloured silk jacket and an olive-green shirt. But he insisted on her trying a mulberry-coloured suit, a scarlet shift, a tangerine two-piece, and a gold lamé cocktail dress, all of which looked fantastic.

By the time she had acquired all the necessary accessories, it was time to go up to their suite to change for dinner.

They were followed by a small retinue of hotel staff who carried the various bags, boxes and packages, and for the first time Cassandra knew what it felt like to be married to a rich man.

When everything had been taken through to the bedroom, she thanked them, and as they left Lang tipped each and every one with his usual generosity.

'I've a couple of phone calls to make,' he told her, when they were alone, 'so if you'd like to go ahead and get ready?'

When her purchases had been unpacked, a little dazed at having such a choice, she glanced through the open door and, finding Lang between calls, asked, 'What shall I wear?'

'Why not make it the gold lamé?'

Everything laid out neatly on the bed, she went into the bathroom to take a quick shower.

Dried and perfumed, she slipped on an ivory satin robe and loosely looped the belt. She had just finished pulling a brush through her tangle of curls when Lang walked in.

His eyes swept her from head to toe, lingering where the satin clung, gleaming and seductive, to every curve.

She replaced the brush and, obeying an impulse, went over to him. Putting her arms around his neck, she stood on tiptoe to kiss him. As she did so the belt slipped undone and the robe's satin edges parted enticingly.

He went white to the lips. With a sudden savage movement that took her by surprise, he unwound her arms and thrust her away from him so violently that she staggered back against the shower stall.

As, a hand to her mouth, her eyes wide and startled,

she stared at him, he demanded with cold fury, 'What the *hell* do you think you're playing at?'

'I—I don't know what you mean,' she stammered. 'I just wanted to thank you for—'

'I've no need for thanks.'

'Well, perhaps I feel the need to give them.'

With icy contempt, he said, 'A verbal thank-you would have been quite sufficient. You've no need to act like…like a whore.'

'How dare you?' Dragging the robe together, she fastened the belt with shaking hands. 'I'm your *wife*.'

'And, as I've already told you, I regard it as a husband's prerogative to buy his wife's clothes. I don't need payment.'

Her own face pinched and white, she cried, '*Payment*! I had no intention of trying to *pay* you. And I wasn't thanking you so much for the clothes as for the *interest* you took.'

The words tumbling over each other, she went on, 'Back in London, when I bought my trousseau, Alan refused to come with me. I asked him, didn't he care how I looked? His answer was that he hated shopping, and had no intention of hanging around looking like a fool while I tried things on. He said that so long as I was well turned out, and didn't let him down, he wasn't the slightest bit concerned what I chose. Such lack of interest felt like a slap in the face…

'But *you* were different. I was so pleased and happy that you seemed to care what I wore and how I looked—' She broke off abruptly, close to tears, her pleasure totally spoilt.

Head down, she didn't see Lang's expression change from anger and contempt to regret and compunction.

Biting back the urge to weep, she lifted her chin and, without looking at him, started for the bedroom.

'Wait…' He caught hold of her arm.

Tearing herself free, she cried, 'Take your hands off me.'

In the bedroom she pushed aside her new finery and, her back turned to him, pulled on the clothes she'd been wearing previously. Then, with no idea of where she was going or what she intended to do, her only thought to get away, she headed for the door.

CHAPTER NINE

'WAIT, Cassandra! I want to talk to you.'

When she ignored the injunction, he followed her, and, grasping her wrist, turned her back into his arms.

She fought furiously. 'Let me go; I don't want you to touch me.'

But, without hurting her, he kept her where she was, saying evenly, 'If you'll calm down and just listen a minute…'

He took both her hands and led her to a chair. Pushing her gently into it, he said, 'I think we could both use a pre-dinner drink. What would you like?'

Unable to find her voice, she half shook her head.

He went over to the sideboard, and returned a moment later with a glass of sherry which he put into her hand. Then, having poured a whisky and soda for himself, he sat down close by and looked at her.

Leaning forward, he put a finger to her lips. 'I want to apologize for saying what I did.'

'You were quite wrong.'

'I realize that now, and believe me, I'm sorry.'

The bitter hurt implicit in her voice, she said, 'I just don't understand how you could think a thing like that.'

Heavily, he told her, 'Because it's happened to me before.' Almost to himself, he added, 'But I shouldn't have presumed that you were tarred with the same brush…'

Then, with a determined attempt to lighten the mood, he said, 'Now what about putting on your new dress? We'll have dinner at Jordan's, before we go and paint the town red.'

Trying hard to regain her composure, she rose to do his bidding. But she'd never felt less like going out. The gold lamé dress that previously she'd looked forward to wearing no longer held any appeal. Neither did the thought of painting the town.

After a glance at her face he stretched out a hand and kept her there. 'Forget it. If we're to have the slightest chance of enjoying our honeymoon, I owe you an explanation... Maybe it's time I told you about Nina.' Then he said decidedly, 'But let's have dinner first.'

'I'm not very hungry.'

He frowned his disapproval. 'You had no breakfast and hardly any lunch, so you must try to eat something... Do you want to go down, or would you prefer to stay here?'

'I'd prefer to stay here.'

He nodded, and a moment later was lifting the phone and asking for a light meal to be sent up.

A dinner-trolley arrived with admirable speed and efficiency, and in a very few minutes they were sitting down to watercress soup, grilled chicken and artichoke hearts.

In truth, Cassandra's appetite was non-existent, but when the food was placed in front of her she made an effort to eat enough to satisfy Lang.

He himself ate sparingly, his expression grim, abstracted, as if his thoughts were far from pleasant.

As though he sat in a spotlight, she found herself very aware of him, of the small jagged scar on his left temple, the little laughter lines around his eyes, the fan of long, curly lashes, incongruous in such a tough, masculine face.

Watching him with heightened sensibilities, she noticed the neat, almost fastidious way he ate his food, the angle he held his fork, how from time to time he rested a wrist on the edge of the trolley...

Glancing up suddenly, he caught her eye.

Feeling herself start to blush, she looked hastily away.

'Coffee?' he queried evenly.

'Please.'

Having filled two cups, he carried them over to the low table, before returning to pull out her chair.

When she would have taken a seat in one of the armchairs, he drew her on to the settee and sat down beside her.

She heard his sigh and saw that his face held the bleakness of winter. Whatever he was about to tell her, it was going to cost him dearly...

'Lang.' With sudden compassion, she touched his hand. 'If it's something you'd rather not talk about, please don't... I know you loved Nina, and if your marriage wasn't perfect—'

Flatly, he said, 'I didn't love Nina...'

I didn't love Nina... Cassandra's glow of relief was followed by guilt. How *could* she be pleased that he hadn't loved his first wife? It was cruel and unfeeling...

But he was going on. 'Our marriage was hell from the word go. I've never spoken about it before. Not even to Rob...though he must have guessed how things were.'

There was a pause, as though he was steeling himself, before he continued abruptly, 'I was living in Beverly Hills when Nina and I first met. I'd been invited to a Hollywood party by a film producer who was hoping Dalton International would provide some financial backing for his next project. She was a house guest there.

'Nina was a very beautiful woman, a true blonde with a stunning figure and eyes like aquamarines. She came from a good background, and could have taken her pick of the smart set's most eligible men.

'As far as her family were concerned, I was more of a rough diamond, and I was flattered when she made a dead set at me.

'Though her home was in San Francisco she stayed over in Hollywood and I began to take her out. Nina was polished, and clever socially, a modern woman who knew exactly what she wanted and how to get it.

'I'd expected her to be free-thinking, sexually unin-hibited, but though she was fond of teasing, of leading me on, she always stopped short of going to bed.

'We'd been going out for a week or so when she told me I was special, that she'd fallen in love with me. She made it clear that before we slept together she wanted marriage, my ring on her finger...'

Sitting with her hands clasped tightly together, Cassandra listened with almost painful intensity.

'Used to modern excesses, I saw her unwillingness to make love until we were married as a rare kind of purity, a sign of self-respect. I imagined she was curbing her natural instincts, her warmth and passion.

'I was nearly thirty; I wanted a real home and a fam-ily. I thought she would make the ideal wife and mother, and *she loved me*. What more could any man ask...?'

Cassandra bit her lip. Lang had once said that his half-sister was the only person in the world who had ever cared a damn for him. To someone who had needed love as much as he did, it must have seemed like a dream come true.

'After the wedding I was swiftly disillusioned, as all fools must surely be. Nina might not have slept with *me*, but she'd certainly had plenty of other lovers. I'd been quite wrong to presume that she was as pure as driven snow—' his mouth twisted in a wry attempt at humour '—but I soon found that as far as I was concerned she was the original ice queen.

'Instead of warmth, there was coolness. Instead of passion, indifference. Instead of love, expediency and avarice.'

His voice grew harsh. 'Her father, I discovered, had made a series of disastrous investments that had brought him to the verge of disgrace and bankruptcy, so to save the family name she had married the richest dope she could find.

'She didn't love me, she didn't even *want* me. As far as Nina was concerned, sex was a weapon, a means of getting her own way. She used it as an inducement, withheld it as a punishment, or amused herself by blowing hot and cold to prove her power.

'After I'd bailed her father out, or provided her with a new wardrobe, or a diamond necklace, or whatever else she demanded, I was *rewarded*...'

Cassandra winced. It was becoming only too plain why he'd acted as he had, and why he'd been angry last night when he'd thought *she* was blowing hot and cold.

'When, on ethical grounds, I wouldn't buy her a mink coat, as a sign of her displeasure, she refused to sleep with me. After several weeks of getting the cold shoulder I gave her an ultimatum. Either she stopped that kind of behaviour or I wanted a legal separation.

'It didn't take her long to decide she'd prefer to be the wife of a wealthy man, rather than out on a limb. She said that if I would double her allowance, and move to San Francisco—she hated the smog and heat of LA— she would do her best to make our marriage work... But the deal didn't include having children.

'I thought if we could really get it together she might change her mind. So I bought a house in The Bay area and we made a fresh start.

'However, things soon began to go wrong. She was hardly ever at home, especially in the evenings. Eventually she began staying out overnight. I made it clear I wasn't going to stand for it, and she blew her top, saying she was entitled to have friends. But I was fairly sure she was two-timing me.

'Then the gutter press got hold of the story and printed a photograph of Nina and a playboy property developer named Van Roc together at a nightclub. They followed that with one of me as ''the cuckolded husband'', and had a great time digging for dirt...'

No wonder he'd been so bitter about grapevine gossip, Cassandra thought sadly.

'Roc was a married man with children, so it must have been hell for his wife... When I told Nina it had to stop, she vehemently denied they were anything more than friends, and for a while was a great deal more circumspect.

'About two months later I read in the paper that he was in serious financial difficulties over a new shopping complex he was building. Nina and I still shared a room, but she'd been very cool and distant and we hadn't slept together for weeks. That night she turned on the heat and tried sexual persuasion to cajole me into giving him a huge loan.

'When I refused, we had a blazing row, during which she admitted that they *had* been having an affair, and taunted me with the fact that they'd been lovers even before we were married. She said he was a fantastic lover, worth two of me, and that she'd only pressured me into moving to San Francisco to be closer to him.

'To be honest, I no longer cared. I kept on paying her allowance, and she took a flat in downtown 'Frisco. I didn't want to stay trapped in a marriage that had been nothing but a worthless, degrading sham, so, though I hated the idea, I began divorce proceedings.'

There was a long, painful pause, and Cassandra had just decided he was going to say no more when, with an obvious effort, he went on, 'Nina had been gone about three months when I got home one night to find her waiting naked in my bed. She said she wanted to come back to me. I asked, What about Roc? She told me it was all over between them. Finished.

'She begged for another chance, said that she'd been foolish to leave me, that she did want children after all.

If only I'd take her back we could start a family and be happy together...

'But I had no intention of jumping on that merry-go-round again, so I turned down her offer, and told her to get out.'

His face ashen, he added, 'Though I didn't know it then, my refusal signed her death warrant.'

Aghast, Cassandra breathed, 'She didn't...?'

'Commit suicide? No. She wasn't the kind to take her own life.'

'Well, whatever happened, you can't blame yourself—'

But as though she hadn't spoken he ploughed on. 'Three evenings later the police contacted me. That afternoon her car had been found by the side of the interstate, with her body inside it.

'There wasn't a mark on her. They were puzzled because she'd died from loss of blood, which suggested internal injuries, but the car wasn't even scratched.

'The post-mortem examination showed that earlier on the day she died she'd had an abortion and something had gone terribly wrong. She must have felt faint while she was driving and pulled over.'

Horrified, Cassandra whispered, 'She was pregnant when she came to see you?'

'That was why she wanted me to take her back—so she could pass the child off as mine...'

No wonder he seemed so bitter at times. How could any woman be heartless enough to refuse to have his children, then try to palm another man's child off on him?

'Later I discovered, through a letter she'd kept, that when Roc found out about the baby, instead of leaving his wife, as she'd hoped, he told her he'd been intending to end their affair.

'His wife, who was pregnant with their fourth child, had had enough. She was threatening to take the children and leave him, unless he toed the marital line. He advised Nina either to go back to me and pretend the baby was mine, or have an abortion.

'When the first option failed, she went for the second. But, apparently afraid of it getting into the papers, instead of going to a reputable clinic, she went out of town to some hole-and-corner place where nobody knew who she was...

'It was ironical really,' he added bitterly. 'The pathologist's findings made front-page news... As you can imagine, the press hounded me for weeks, asking endless offensive questions...'

He dropped his head in his hands. 'But the worst part was I felt, and still feel, partly to blame both for Nina's death and the child's.'

Her stomach tying itself in a knot, Cassandra recalled Rob's words. 'Even Lang, who's the most stable of men, took Nina's death very badly. He's still cut up over it...'

Then Lang himself, saying, 'Perhaps my conscience already carries a big enough burden...'

And all this for a woman who had never cared a jot for him, who had only tried to use him.

Filled with anger, and an urgent need to ease some of his pain, Cassandra jumped to her feet. Praying that shock tactics would be more effective than any amount of sympathy, she said crisply, 'Well, I've certainly changed my mind!'

Lang lifted his head and looked at her. Sounding a little fuddled, he asked, 'About what?'

The die was cast. 'Earlier today I said I wouldn't call you a fool, but now I've changed my mind. If you believe that you are in any degree to blame for your first wife's death, then you're a bigger fool than even *she* took you for!'

Watching that look of despair and desolation give way to a kind of startled incredulity, she rushed on, 'She and her lover were the *only* people responsible. When her attempt to saddle you with another man's child failed, she didn't *have* to have an abortion. It was her own choice. Some women in a similar situation would have opted to keep the child and go it alone.'

As he opened his mouth to speak, Cassandra demanded, 'Tell me something; if she'd been honest and told you about the baby, would you have taken her back?'

'No.' His answer was unequivocal.

'Would you have suggested she have an abortion?'

'Certainly not.'

'What if she'd decided to keep the child? Would you have helped her financially?'

'Of course.'

'Even though it wasn't yours? Why should *you* feel any sense of responsibility when her lover didn't? If anyone should feel in any way to blame for what happened, surely it should be on *his* conscience, not yours.'

'Yes. I know all that,' Lang said wearily. 'The thing I can't forgive myself for is that last night. I should have guessed from her desperation that something was seriously wrong... But I let her leave without even trying to find out what it was.'

So that was his real hang-up.

Her face white and set, Cassandra cried, 'What if you *had* tried...? Do you imagine for one minute that she would have told you?

'Instead of allowing emotions to get in the way, think about it logically. She'd taunted you with this fantastic lover of hers... Can you honestly believe she would have admitted that he'd abandoned her when she needed him most? Admitted *why* she'd tried to seduce you? Like hell she would! Her pride wouldn't have let her!'

Then, throwing any last shreds of caution to the wind, she said, 'In my opinion it's high time you saw it as it was and stopped wallowing in unnecessary guilt. High time you made an effort to put the whole thing behind you—' Running out of breath, she came to an abrupt stop.

He got to his feet and stood looking down at her, his face a taut mask, apart from a little tic at the corner of his mouth. 'Well, well, well… Now I know exactly what it feels like to be taken by the scruff of the neck and shaken.'

Suddenly losing her confidence, wishing she'd stayed silent, Cassandra stammered, 'I—I'm sorry.'

He smiled thinly. 'It may turn out to be a very salutary experience… Though I'm not sure I take kindly to the word ''wallowing''.'

'Perhaps I shouldn't have said what I did,' she began unhappily, 'but I couldn't bear to see you torturing yourself like that, and I…'

Her apology tailed off as he turned his back and walked to the door. A moment later the latch clicked quietly behind him, leaving her bitterly regretting her scathing remarks, her attempt to shock him into a new awareness.

By choosing the wrong tactics, she had totally alienated him. Now it was too late she could see that it wasn't yet possible to shrug off the past. He was a strong man, but he'd been tried to the limit, and beyond, by the traumatic circumstances of his wife's death.

Sitting staring blindly into space, Cassandra thought about all she'd learnt. What he'd told her had made a lot of things clear, but it had left one very important question unanswered.

How did *she* fit into the equation?

With one unhappy marriage behind him, why had he embarked on a second that seemed to stand as little chance of success?

She remembered how he had stressed the fact that she might be pregnant. Was he afraid of history repeating itself?

No, it couldn't be that. When he'd broached the subject she had told him unequivocally that she wouldn't consider abortion.

In any case, she reminded herself, the whole thing had all been carefully planned long before she'd slept with him. Perhaps he'd been speaking the exact truth when he'd called her an obsession.

But obsessions died. If she was nothing more than that, why had he insisted on marriage rather than an affair?

Sighing, Cassandra admitted that it made no more sense now than when she'd first thought it through.

But there *had* to be a reason. Suppose—she felt her blood run cold—suppose it was some kind of role reversal? His first wife had made his life hell. Was he bitter enough to want to take it out on his second? Make *her* a whipping-boy for *Nina*?

The notion had a weird kind of logic and, her breath caught in her throat, she began to tremble violently.

It was a full minute before she could pull herself together enough to dismiss the crazy thought. That was the sort of thing you might read in a book, not the sort of thing that happened in real life.

But truth could be stranger than fiction... She already had proof of that...

No, she was being utterly ridiculous. Lang wasn't some kind of monster, just a man who had been badly hurt and was still suffering.

Her failure to help him had left her dismayed and utterly wretched. It grieved her to think he was still on the rack, *mattered* that she had let him down. If she had loved him it couldn't have mattered more...

How long she sat there, her thoughts going round and round like a squirrel in a cage, she was never sure. But, finally waking to the realization that it must be an hour or more since Lang had left, depressed and tired, stiff from remaining in one position, she went to bed.

At two o'clock in the morning she was still tossing

and turning restlessly, unable to sleep, when there was a faint sound from the outer room. A moment later the bedroom door quietly opened and closed.

'Still awake?' Lang's voice was even.

'Yes.' She barely breathed the word.

He came and sat on the edge of the bed. His thick blond hair was rumpled and his shirt open at the neck. The room was light enough for her to be able to see a faint sheen of sweat on his forehead.

'Lang, where have you been?'

'Walking.' His expression was calm and relaxed. As she gazed up at him, he took her hand and, lifting it to his lips, kissed the palm.

She made a small sound between a sigh and a sob. 'I'm sorry.'

He shook his head. 'You've nothing to be sorry for. Just the opposite, in fact. It needed shock tactics to make me really listen.

'I'd become so used to the idea that I could have *altered* things... But you were absolutely right. Even if I *had* asked Nina what was wrong, she would never have told me...'

Putting a palm against Cassandra's cheek, he added, 'Now I'm convinced of that, I can stop thinking "if only" and start enjoying our honeymoon.'

He looked like a man who had had a great weight lifted from his shoulders, and a corresponding weight lifted from hers.

Smiling up at him, she asked softly, 'How far did you walk?'

'About twelve miles.'

'Oh... I expect you're tired?'

'Not too tired.' A gleam in his eye, he added, 'I've always considered honeymoons were meant to be enjoyed to the full.' Then, with wry self-mockery, he said, 'Not to say wallowed in.'

*   *   *

The following weeks were some of the happiest Cassandra had ever known. Determinedly pushing away all thoughts of the past, and worries about the future, she enjoyed every moment of their honeymoon.

They went out and about, spending long sunny days travelling, and in a very short time Cassandra was fit and tanned and glowing, her ash-brown hair streaked with gold that Lang told her was like tangled sunshine.

He himself was looking younger and happier and carefree. Seeing the change, Rob, who at their insistence had once or twice made up a threesome, was delighted, and said so.

But though Cassandra's days were full of pleasure she found herself waiting impatiently for the nights. Wonderful nights spent in Lang's arms, sometimes just talking companionably, more often than not making long, delectable love.

Lang called her darling, told her she was beautiful and exciting, warm and sweet and sexy, a delight to make love to, but the three words she hoped to hear were never spoken.

When she discovered that she wasn't pregnant, at first her feelings were mixed. Then she told herself firmly that it was just as well. Though the present held almost everything she could have hoped for, the future remained uncertain.

It was almost the end of their honeymoon—Penny would be arriving the next day—and Cassandra was no nearer to solving the mystery of why Lang had coerced her into marrying him.

During the preceding weeks she had resolutely banished the puzzle to the back of her mind, but it was always there, like a shadow lying in wait to ambush her whenever she relaxed her guard.

Now, sitting on the penthouse terrace in the relative cool of late evening, waiting for Lang to finish a call and join her, it crept into her consciousness once more, bringing with it a sudden memory of Alan.

She sighed, guiltily aware that she had never given him a thought. Poor Alan. Comparing him to Lang, she could see how narrow and joyless he'd been, a man with little warmth and no sense of humour.

Recalling how close she'd been to marrying him, she shivered...

'Something wrong?'

She jumped almost guiltily. For so big a man, Lang moved lithely, quietly, and she hadn't heard him coming.

'No... No, of course not.'

Dropping into the lounger beside her, he queried, 'Then why were you looking like someone about to face the electric chair?'

'I was just thinking,' she said evasively.

He picked it up immediately. 'About what?'

Unwilling to mention Alan, she hesitated.

Lang's mouth tightened ominously. 'As you're so reluctant to tell me, I can only presume you were thinking about Brent.'

Her flush was answer enough.

'What's the matter, still missing him? Still wishing *he* was your husband? I must say you've done a good job of disguising the fact that his ghost shares our bed—'

'It does nothing of the kind,' she broke in desperately. 'And far from missing him, or wishing he was my husband, I've never given him a thought until now. And if you want to know exactly what I *was* thinking, it was that with hindsight I can see just what a terrible mistake marrying him would have been. Trapped in a totally loveless—'

'But it wouldn't have been totally loveless,' Lang broke in smoothly. 'He might not have loved you, but you told me more than once that you loved him.'

After a moment, she admitted, 'I realize now that I was mistaken. I don't think I ever really loved him.'

Incautiously, she added, 'Perhaps what I did feel was a kind of gratitude…'

Lang's well-marked brows went up. 'Gratitude? Why *gratitude*?'

'It's not easy to explain,' she said weakly.

'Try.'

'Well, I—I felt safe with Alan. Though it was clear he was attracted, he didn't put me under pressure or pose any threat…'

'You mean sexually?'

'Yes.'

Lang steepled his fingers and waited.

She stumbled on, 'I—I'd lost confidence. While I was still a student I had a rather traumatic experience that made me wary of men.'

'Do go on,' he said inexorably.

'It's not something I like to talk about. Can't we just leave it?'

'No, I don't think we can.' Lang disagreed softly. 'It's time you told me about Sean.'

Her green eyes wide and startled, she asked, 'How do you know about Sean?'

'Surely you remember Brent mentioned him that night?'

But not by name.

As though reading her unspoken thought, Lang told her, 'Later, when we were having a drink in the bar, he brought the subject up again. He hinted that your past might be far from spotless…'

Cassandra felt a fleeting surprise. Though Alan had certainly been angry enough to want to blacken her, she wouldn't have thought he was brave enough to chance annoying Lang by disparaging his new bride.

But he must have been, otherwise how would Lang have known Sean's name?

With an edge to his voice that she hadn't heard for weeks, Lang was continuing, 'So if you'd like to start

from the beginning and give me your version? Tell me
how and when you and Sean got to know one another.'

Now it was too late, she wished she'd told him earlier
of her own free will, rather than having it dragged out
of her.

CHAPTER TEN

HER face pale, and with a despairing feeling that she'd already been tried and found guilty, Cassandra began jerkily, 'It was towards the end of my second year at college. We met at the theatre. I'd been given a ticket by another student who couldn't go.

'Sean and I had neighbouring seats, and somehow we got talking. He bought me a drink during the interval. When the show ended it was pouring with rain and I hadn't a mac. He offered me a lift back to college.

'The following day, after classes, he turned up with tickets for a play I'd mentioned I'd like to see. From then on he was a regular visitor.'

'And a welcome one, I gather?'

Ignoring any snideness, she went on, 'Sean was tall, dark, handsome, and charming, any woman's dream. He dressed well, drove an expensive car, knew all the best bars and restaurants in town, and seemed to like lashing his money about.

'It was a change from penny-pinching, and at first I enjoyed it... Then I began to feel uncomfortable, to worry about him spending so much on me. But whenever I tried to refuse a meal or a gift or an outing he wouldn't hear of it. He said it was his pleasure to buy me things.'

Bitterly, she added, 'All the girls envied me like mad. Except Penny. For some reason she never really took to him.

'Before long he wanted us to become lovers...' Cassandra's voice faltered, and she stopped speaking.

Making it a statement rather than a question, Lang
prodded, 'But you didn't.'

She shook her head.

'Why not, if he was as handsome and charming as
you say?'

'I don't really know,' she admitted honestly. 'Something held me back.'

'Even though you were still letting him spend his
money on you?' There was censure in both Lang's voice
and his expression.

'I told you, I *tried* to stop him, but he wouldn't take
no for an answer—'

'Had you any idea where all this money came from?'
Lang cut in sharply.

'I thought at first he must have a very good job. But
when I asked him what he did he said he didn't need to
work; his father had died and left him well off...'

'Go on.'

Memories crowded in, cruel and sharp as barbed wire.
'He was pressing me hard to sleep with him. He'd become so intense...obsessed almost... I was starting to
feel stifled, threatened, and I'd begun to dread the
thought of seeing him...

'I couldn't concentrate and my work was suffering.
Penny suggested that I simply told him to get lost. But
he'd spent so much on me that I felt trapped...
indebted... I was trying to find a kind way to end things
when I discovered he was married—'

'You mean you didn't know before?' Lang demanded
sharply.

'Of course not.' A shade helplessly, she admitted,
'Though we'd been going out for weeks I knew hardly
anything about him. If ever I tried to find out more, he
changed the subject—'

'So how did you discover he was a married man?'

'Quite by accident. Penny and I shared a unit in the
hall of residence, and occasionally, if it wasn't too late

when he took me back, and I knew she was home, I let him come in for a coffee.

'That particular night he'd pushed a small concert programme into his pocket. As he was fishing it out to verify some point he was making, he dropped an envelope addressed to Mr and Mrs Sean Bonington.

'When he realized I'd seen it, he admitted that he had a wife, but he said he didn't love her, it was me he wanted.

'I felt dreadful about the whole thing, and deeply sorry for his wife. My only consolation was that I'd never slept with him.'

A warm night breeze blew a tendril of hair across her cheek and she tucked it behind her ear before going on. 'I told him that it was all over between us and I never wanted to see him again. I asked him to leave.'

His face showing no emotion, Lang asked, 'But that wasn't the end of it?'

'No. He came back the next night and the next. I wouldn't let him in, and I refused to answer his calls or read his letters. But instead of giving up he started to hang around the college...'

She shuddered. 'The next few weeks were a nightmare. If it hadn't been for Penny I think I'd have cracked. She went everywhere with me, and never left me alone for a minute.'

'If it was like you say, why didn't you tell the authorities?'

'Penny said I should, but I didn't want to get him into trouble because of his wife... And I couldn't help but feel it was partly my own fault for not realizing sooner where things were leading...

'Then one afternoon, coming out of classes, we turned a corner and there he was. Before I'd got over the shock, Penny waded in. Normally she's so honest it hurts, and I'd never known her to tell a lie. But this time she lied like a trooper. She told him that his behaviour had been reported, and if he was found on the premises again Security would pick him up and call the police, and I would press charges.

'That seemed to do the trick. He turned and walked away without a word, and we both breathed a sigh of relief.

'At the end of the school year we were given the chance to rent a small flat. After living in student accommodation for two years we were only too pleased to take it.

'One night, a few weeks after we'd moved in, there was a knock at the door. Penny was out, and I answered. It was Sean...

'I was just starting to feel safe, and seeing him standing there was a nasty shock. The chain was on, but he'd put his foot in the door so I couldn't close it.

'When I asked him how he knew where I was living, he admitted he'd followed me home. He said he'd realized how stupid he'd been, and wanted to apologize.

'He told me he and his wife were moving up to Manchester, and before they went he'd like me to have a drink with him for old times' sake, and to show there were no hard feelings. He was carrying a bottle of champagne, and he sounded genuine. Like a fool I let him in...

'The minute he got inside, he changed. He caught hold of me and started to kiss me. When I tried to fight him off, he called me a frigid bitch and said I was driving him wild...

'If Penny hadn't come back when she did—' Cassandra stopped abruptly, racked by shudders.

There was dead silence.

Hoping for a kind word...a trace of support or understanding...*something*, she looked up.

Lang sat a little aloof, watching her. The warm, carefree man of the past month was gone, in his place a hard-eyed stranger who showed no sign of understanding and offered no comfort.

Hoarsely, she said, 'You think the same as Alan, that I led Sean on, used him, and then got scared when he wanted to collect...'

'Isn't that how it was?'

She felt a kind of dull hopelessness. If that was what he believed, what use would it be to deny it?

'Isn't it?' he persisted.

'Ask Penny,' she suggested wearily.

Coolly, he assured her, 'I fully intend to.'

It took a moment or two to sink in, then she said slowly, 'So that was why you asked her to come over.'

'I'm sure Miss Lane will enjoy her visit and it saved me having to go to London.'

Shaken by the *intent*, Cassandra said uncertainly, 'I can't see why something that's over and done with matters so much. Why you needed to go to those lengths.'

'I wanted to know what happened between you and Sean.'

'I've told you what happened.'

'As Brent remarked, you could be making your own side right. I would prefer an unbiased version.'

'Are you sure you'll get one from Penny?'

'As a loyal friend, I'm sure she'll stick up for you, but I'm equally confident of being able to read between the lines and end up with the truth.'

White to the lips, Cassandra asked scornfully, 'And what then? Will *you* forgive me?'

'That stung, didn't it? I watched your face when Brent was sounding so noble...

'And no, if it turns out that you knew Sean was married and you still led him on for what you could get out of him, I'll never forgive you.'

Trenchantly, he added, 'You see, it would make you the same kind of woman as my first wife.'

She sat quite still, while every drop of blood in her

body seemed to turn to ice. So, far from being the idyll it had seemed, their honeymoon had been nothing but a sham.

Rather than being happy and enjoying her company, as she'd fondly imagined, Lang's apparent insouciance had stemmed simply from relief that he no longer felt any guilt over Nina's death.

Like her, he had had hidden reservations, a dark question, lodged at the back of his mind.

Finding her voice somehow, she said, 'You've known about Sean since you talked to Alan. If you feel so strongly, why haven't you brought it up before?'

'I was rather hoping you'd tell me of your own free will.'

'On our wedding night I almost did. But it isn't something I like to remember or talk about, and...'

'And?' he prompted, when she paused.

With difficulty, she said, 'It occurred to me that you might see it the same way as Alan... And I was right...'

Mockingly, he said, 'You sound reproachful.'

She hit back. 'Perhaps I shouldn't have hoped for trust from a man who's been warped by his first marriage.' Then she said bitterly, 'I'd have to get Sean himself to admit the truth before you'd believe it... And I doubt if he'd do that, even if I knew where to find him.'

Curtly, Lang asked, 'Then you don't know what happened to him?'

She shook her head. 'He'd mentioned moving north... I suppose he did. I never tried to find out. All I wanted to do was blot him from my mind...'

But like some vengeful phantom his ghost had returned to spoil her honeymoon, to threaten any faint chance of happiness, or of making her marriage work.

There was a long silence, heavy with shattered images and disappointed hopes.

'About ready for bed?' Lang's voice was studiously casual.

Cassandra glanced up. His expression was neither friendly nor unfriendly; it merely held a kind of *waiting*.

'Yes, I'm ready,' she said tonelessly, and rose to her feet.

'What a docile little wife,' he taunted. 'Aren't you going to refuse to sleep with me? Insist on moving into the other room in case I want to make love to you?'

'No.'

'Anxious to prove you're not like Nina?'

'No. I just don't see the point of cutting off my nose to spite my face.'

She saw her answer had startled him, as she'd intended it to.

'My, my,' he murmured admiringly, 'while this kind of spirit lasts it should prove to be fun.'

But his searching glance at her pale face suggested he had guessed her real feelings and was merely mocking her bravado.

An arm around her waist in a parody of togetherness, he led her inside.

'Would you like to use our shower? I'll have the spare one.'

During the past weeks they had got into the pleasurable habit of showering together, and his rejection of this intimacy chilled her, but, refusing to show it, she agreed, 'Yes, I don't mind.'

When she emerged some ten minutes later, dried and perfumed, wearing the satin robe over her nightdress, her sun-streaked hair in a cloud around her shoulders, he was already in bed.

At the sight of him lying with just a sheet drawn up to his waist, his hands clasped behind his blond head, she swallowed hard.

'Come here.'

The arrogant command brought a faint flush of apricot to her cheekbones, but, well aware that he was testing her mettle, she went and sat on the edge of the bed.

He looked up at her, dark blue eyes gleaming between thick lashes. 'Feel free to kiss me.'

She tried hard to keep her cool. 'Thanks, but I'm not sure I want to.'

'Changed your mind about the spare room?'

'You sound as if you *want* me to go. Or do you just want the pleasure of telling me I'm like Nina?'

'I was simply giving you another chance.'

'How kind of you. But, practically speaking, it wouldn't be worth the effort of moving. By tomorrow night Penny will need the spare room.'

He smiled a little. 'Then while you're feeling so enthusiastic about staying, perhaps we could try something different.'

'Something different?' In spite of all her efforts, her voice squeaked.

'Well, I have this fantasy—'

'What kind of fantasy?' she broke in sharply.

'I thought for once you might take the initiative and make love to me.' Watching her change colour, he added softly, 'But if you prefer to go...?'

Wondering why he felt this need to goad and punish her, but determined that she wasn't going to back down, she squared her shoulders. 'Wild horses couldn't drag me away,' she assured him boldly, and watched his expression change from a kind of cynical satisfaction to respect.

'Bravo!' he applauded.

Fighting down her natural shyness, with a kind of fragile dignity, she took off her robe and slid in beside him.

He lay quite still while, propped on one elbow, she trailed little kisses along his jawline and down the strong column of his throat. Her fingertips stroked over the smooth skin of his shoulders and his muscular chest, before following the sprinkle of crisp body hair down to his trim waist and flat stomach. When he still made no move, she hesitated and her hand stilled.

'You don't seem to be putting your heart into it,' he complained.

'You don't seem to be in the right mood,' she retaliated.

He looked at her through half-closed lids. 'On our wedding night you were much more seductive.'

'On our wedding night it was a great deal easier.'

Then, she had *wanted* to arouse him. Now, because of his coolness, and the knowledge that he was just playing with her, it was only bravado, an unwillingness to admit defeat, that kept her there.

'Perhaps if you were to try some verbal blandishments?' he suggested.

'You once said our true forte was non-verbal communication.'

'It is, once we're on the same wavelength. But I've always agreed with D.H. Lawrence that sex isn't just physical, it's mostly in the head. Love too, I strongly suspect. Perhaps if you were to pretend you loved me…?'

'You mean like Nina?'

He didn't even blink. 'Why not? I've learnt not to take declarations of love too seriously.'

Her voice sounding hoarse, impeded, she said, 'I'm afraid I'm not very good at pretence…'

But with sudden blinding insight she knew there was no need for pretence. All the times she had denied loving him, had labelled her feelings as just physical attraction, she had been lying to herself.

From the moment he'd taken her hand and looked into her eyes, though on one level she'd tried hard to resist, she had been lost.

Suddenly, dangerously close to tears, she threw in the towel. 'Perhaps it would be better if I did move into the other room…'

When she made to get out of bed, he caught her wrist. 'Don't go...'

Her voice brittle, she said, 'As I'm hopeless at pretence, and not too hot at seduction, there's not much point in staying.'

He touched his lips to the inside of the wrist he was holding. 'If you give me a bit of cooperation I'll take over and show you how it's done.'

'I'll be happy to give you as much cooperation as you gave me.'

'I thought you weren't going to cut off your nose to spite your face?'

'That was before I realized you just wanted to play with me.'

'Oh, I want a great deal more than that.' Taking her hand, he placed it on his firm flesh. 'Your seduction technique is better than you first imagined. All that's needed now is to make you want me.'

And in that he succeeded easily. But while her body welcomed his her heart shed tears of blood for a love she dared not admit.

Next day, rather than sending a car to meet Penny, Lang suggested that they go in person. Only too pleased, Cassandra agreed, and they drove to the airport in the late afternoon sunshine.

The flight was on time and they'd only been waiting a matter of minutes before Penny appeared, accompanied by one of the cabin crew who was carrying her cases.

When the women had hugged each other, Cassandra introduced the two people she'd suddenly realized were the most important in her life.

Lang took the newcomer's hand. 'I've been looking forward to meeting you, Miss Lane.'

'Won't you call me Penny?'

'If you'll call me Lang.' While he spoke, he studied her coolly.

Penny was short and sturdy, with a snub nose and dark curly hair framing a square-jawed, no-nonsense face. She was saved from plainness by the most beautiful pair of amber eyes. Eyes that met his levelly, and were fearlessly honest.

Apparently liking what he saw, he smiled at her.

Looking more than a little bowled over, she said cheerfully, 'You'll just have to excuse me if I gawp. I've never met a real live millionaire before.'

Lang threw back his head and laughed. 'And I've never met a woman who spoke her mind with such refreshing frankness.'

Taking her luggage from the steward with a word of thanks, he turned and led the way out to the convertible.

When Penny had finished goggling at the spectacular pyramid that flanked the airport, and they were heading back to town, he asked, 'What was the flight like? Are you feeling very tired?'

'It was wonderful, and I'm not at all tired. I had about seven hours' sleep in a real bed. I'm used to travelling economy class, but this time I was looked after as though I was a VIP.'

'Being the guest of a millionaire does have its advantages,' Lang said drily, adding, 'Now, is there anything in particular you'd like to see or do?'

'Anything and everything I can cram in. For me this is the trip of a lifetime.' Penny made no attempt to hide her enthusiasm.

'Well, before we begin some serious sightseeing, there's one thing I'd like to get out of the way...' A challenge in his eyes, Lang glanced at Cassandra, who was sitting by his side.

Understanding that he was going to allow them no chance to confer, she turned to Penny and said steadily, 'Lang would like to know about Sean. I don't find it easy to talk about it, so would you mind telling him what happened?'

Showing no particular surprise at what must have seemed a strange request, Penny said, 'Certainly, if that's what you want.'

Her eyes meeting Lang's through the rear-view mirror, she asked, 'You won't mind if I speak bluntly?'

'Please do,' he urged.

Clearly and concisely, she began to sketch in the story Cassandra had already told, adding, 'In the circumstances I'm sorry to have to say it, but I neither liked nor trusted Sean. I could never fathom why Cass went out with him in the first place—'

'You don't think it was because he had money?'

Bristling, Penny said, 'If you can even joke about it, you don't know her very well. She did her best to stop him spending his money on her, but he wouldn't listen. He was absolutely obsessed. It was like a sickness, it wasn't *normal*. No wonder she started to feel scared...

'I advised her to give him the push, but she had scruples. She was looking for the kindest way to end it when she discovered he was married—'

'How?'

'An envelope addressed to Mr and Mrs fell out of his pocket.'

'Did Cassandra tell you about it?'

'No, I heard the whole thing. I was in the next room and the walls were like paper.'

'Neither of you knew until then?'

'No. Cass would never have looked at a married man. She was horrified, and asked him to leave. He refused to go, and there was a terrible scene. At the finish I came out of the bedroom and threatened to call Security. So he went...

'I'd been only too right in thinking he was unbalanced. Instead of giving up, he began to lie in wait and stalk her. I was convinced he was dangerous, and it was pretty scary. Then one day we all three came face to face. I threatened him with the police and told him to lay off.

'Unfortunately that wasn't the end of it. Cass and I had taken a flat together, and one night when I got home Sean was there. She'd been gullible enough to let him in...'

Penny gave a shiver, before going on, 'Thank the Lord I had a boyfriend with me who was a rugby forward. We were just in time to save her from being raped. We called the police and an ambulance—'

'An ambulance?'

'She'd tried to fight him off, and he'd beaten her up so badly that she had to spend five days in hospital.'

'Dear God.' Lang sounded shaken.

'You didn't know about that?'

'No, I didn't,' Lang answered almost curtly. 'Was he jailed?'

'No. He should have been, but Cass refused to press charges because of his wife.'

There was a tense silence before, sounding more normal, Lang said, 'Not a very pretty story, but thank you for telling me...'

Then, with a complete change of subject, he said, 'I understand from Cassandra that you share her passion for Westerns?'

Penny grinned. 'Yup.'

'Then tomorrow I suggest we hire some horses and ride through Red Rock Canyon to an Old West town where, to re-create Nevada's past, gunfights are staged...'

For the rest of the journey the two discussed outings and holiday plans, with Lang breaking off from time to time to point out things of special interest, and Penny exclaiming in wonder over each new spectacle.

When they reached the Golden Phoenix, apparently running out of superlatives, she merely gazed around the palatial foyer while her mouth formed an O.

Lang passed the luggage to a bell-hop and, turning to Cassandra, suggested, 'If you'd like to take Penny up, I'll ask Rob to make up a foursome for a night on the town. Say half an hour?'

As soon as the two women were alone in the penthouse, Penny exclaimed, 'I hadn't guessed the half of it! And you didn't tell me this new husband of yours was drop-dead gorgeous...'

Opening her case, she took out a black cocktail dress. 'Will this do?' Then, without waiting for an answer, she asked, 'By the way, who is Rob?'

'He's an old friend of Lang's. I think you'll like him.'

'I'm *dying* to know *everything,* but as we haven't got long I suppose we'd better get ready first...'

Some twenty minutes later, her hair in an elegant chignon and wearing the gold lamé dress Lang had bought her, Cassandra tapped on the guest-room door.

Throwing it open, Penny whistled appreciatively. 'Look at you! Every inch the wife of a millionaire... Is everyone waiting?'

'No, Rob isn't here yet, and Lang's just getting dressed.'

'In that case I'll finish my unpacking.'

Cassandra sat on the bed and watched while the other girl continued to transfer things from her case to the walk-in wardrobe.

After a moment Penny remarked, 'You seem a bit quiet. I hope dragging up all that old business with Sean didn't upset you?'

'No,' Cassandra said with only partial truth. 'I thought it best to clear the air.'

'I was absolutely staggered when I found out! Talk about coincidence! I mean it's almost unbelievable!'

'What's almost unbelievable?'

Putting a pile of underwear in the nearest drawer, Penny said patiently, 'Why, that Sean was Lang's brother-in-law.'

It took several seconds to absorb the shock, but Cassandra never for a moment doubted the truth of that statement. It explained so much.

Through stiff lips, she asked, 'How did you find out?' and was surprised that she sounded so *normal*.

'My office manager, who of course knew all about my trip out here, happened to mention that Lang had come to London about eighteen months ago when his sister and brother-in-law were killed in a car crash...

'Apparently it got into the papers, but we must have missed it somehow—' She stopped speaking as Lang appeared at the open door.

His face was untroubled, his manner relaxed, but some inner knowledge told Cassandra he'd gathered the gist of the conversation.

'Ready to paint the town?' he asked lightly.

'Try me,' Penny answered with enthusiasm.

As they went through to the living-room, Rob appeared. Standing by while the pair were introduced, Cassandra watched Penny's lips form a silent 'Wow!' Rob, she was pleased to see, looked equally smitten.

Lang set himself out to be the perfect host, and the evening, spent dancing and dining and seeing a floor show, proved to be a great success. If Cassandra was a little quiet, no one appeared to notice.

It was almost three o'clock in the morning when Rob queried, 'What about taking in Caesar's Palace next? Then we can go on to the Desert Orchid for a spot of breakfast.'

Penny, still going strong, agreed, 'Sounds fantastic!'

'Why don't you two go?' Lang suggested. 'Cassandra and I are feeling a bit tired.'

'How can anyone feel tired in Las Vegas?' Penny marvelled aloud.

Grinning, Rob pointed out, 'Don't forget they're still on their honeymoon.'

Penny grinned back. 'Of course. Silly of me.'

* * *

The journey back to the Golden Phoenix was made in silence. When they reached the penthouse, Lang slipped the stole from around Cassandra's shoulders and tossed aside his own jacket, before asking, 'Would you like a nightcap?'

She turned to face him squarely. 'I'd like to know why you married me.'

'Can't you guess?'

'It's obviously to do with Sean... But if you blame me for what happened—'

His face cold and set, Lang broke in, 'I don't *now*, but I did *then*... I suppose it's time you knew the whole truth.

'Katy was a brilliant cellist, and she threw up a promising career for Sean, but they hadn't been married very long when he became infatuated with you.

'It wasn't true that his father had left him well off; it was Katy's money he was spending, money I'd given her to buy a house. While he was squandering it on you they were living in a dingy top-floor flat in an otherwise empty building.

'She was six months pregnant when she caught her foot in the threadbare carpet and fell down the stairs. Sean wasn't home. We'll just have to guess where he was. When he finally got back she'd lost the baby.

'When I asked why they hadn't moved out and bought a house, she admitted that most of the money had gone, and she suspected he was either gambling or spending it on another woman. He'd also taken to drinking heavily, presumably because of you.

'She thought things might improve if he was away from London, so I offered to provide a house and a job in Manchester. But when she told him about it he refused to consider moving.

'I decided to find out just what was going on, so I hired a private detective. He gathered all the information I needed—'

'And took that photograph?'

'That's right… But, before I could decide what to do for the best, one night when he'd been drinking heavily Sean crashed the car and killed both himself and Katy—'

Horrified, Cassandra broke in, 'And you blamed me for all that?'

'I thought you were as scheming and heartless as Nina and I wanted to make you pay—not only for what you'd done to Katy, but in the end for what Nina had done to me. A kind of double revenge.

'I wanted to take everything away from you—your fiancé, your job, your home—and then, when the time was right, throw you out.'

'But why *marriage*?' she asked with a kind of desperation. 'And to another woman you felt nothing but hatred and contempt for?'

'Because I'd given up any idea of ever finding love, and marriage provides a much stronger hold.'

'Weren't you afraid that when you threw me out I might ask for alimony?'

He smiled grimly. 'I rather hoped you would. The ensuing battle would have added greatly to my satisfaction.'

Feeling as though she was bleeding to death inside, she said, 'Well, I'm afraid your revenge hasn't proved to be a total success. Marrying Alan would have been a bad mistake, I can find another job of some kind, and I've still got a home with Penny.'

Lifting her chin, she added bitterly, 'And I'm sorry to disappoint you, but I won't be asking for alimony. All I want is my freedom.'

She was about to turn away when he took her shoulders and held her there. 'Where are you going?'

'To pack. If I can get a flight to San Francisco I've still got a ticket home.'

'Don't be foolish, you can't just walk out.'

'If you expect me to play the docile wife until you're ready to dump me—'

'I've no intention of dumping you. That was my original plan.' He sighed. 'Perhaps you were right when you said my first marriage had warped me...'

Then he said, more positively, 'But it didn't take me long to realize I'd been wholly mistaken in thinking you were like Nina... Which made me wonder if I'd been equally mistaken about your relationship with Sean... And now I know the truth—'

'You'll be magnanimous and forgive me?' Cassandra broke in bitterly.

'No. I'll ask *you* to be magnanimous and forgive *me*.'

'And you think you only have to ask?'

'I know I've no right after the way I've treated you, but I need you, Cassandra. I need your warmth and generosity, your humour and your spirit. I need your companionship, some hope for the future...'

His voice dropped to a whisper. 'Please stay with me.'

She had never expected a man like Lang Dalton to beg, and it tore her apart. 'Lang, I—'

Apparently fearing a refusal, he hurried on, 'At least take time to think about it... After all, there's Penny to consider. It would be a shame to deprive her of this "once-in-a-lifetime" holiday. Why not wait and, if you still feel the same, go back with her?'

'I suppose I could,' Cassandra said slowly. 'We'll only be in Las Vegas a few days, and then—'

'Well, she and Rob hit it off so well I thought maybe we could all spend another couple of weeks here.' A gleam in his eyes, he added, 'It's even possible she might not want to go back at all...'

Cassandra felt warmth stealing through her, ousting the chill. 'And while we wait to see I suppose you'll expect me to share your bed?'

'If you can't bring yourself to do that, I'll move out of the penthouse.'

With mock horror, she asked, 'What on earth would the staff think?'

Drawing her against him, he rested his forehead against hers. 'Tonight's been hell. All I could think about was losing you.'

'Would it matter so much?'

'After just these few weeks I can't imagine life without you... I'd even begun to hope that it might turn out to be the kind of fairy tale Penny mentioned...'

Cassandra pursed her lips. 'For a practical woman she has some romantic notions. She even believes in love at first sight.'

'So do I,' he said firmly. 'Though, after giving up all expectations of ever finding love, it took a little while to realize it really *had* happened to me.'

When, choked by joy, she stayed silent, he went on, 'Now all that's needed is the other half of the miracle... At times you've looked at me in a way that made me hope...' Then he said urgently, 'How *do* you feel about me, Cassandra?'

She smiled at him, her heart in her eyes, and promised, 'As in all good fairy tales, when we've been married a year and a day I'll tell you.'

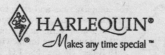

HEART OF THE WEST

Every Man Has His Price!

Lost Springs Ranch was
famous for turning young
mavericks into good men.
So word that the ranch was
in financial trouble sent
a herd of loyal bachelors
stampeding back to
Wyoming to put themselves
on the auction block!

HARLEQUIN®
Makes any time special ™

Visit us at www.romance.net

PHHOWGEN

Back by popular demand are

DEBBIE MACOMBER's

Hard Luck, Alaska, is a
town that needs women!
And the O'Halloran brothers
are just the fellows
to fly them in.

Starting in March 2000 this beloved series returns
in special 2-in-1 collector's editions:

MAIL-ORDER MARRIAGES, featuring
Brides for Brothers and *The Marriage Risk*
On sale March 2000

FAMILY MEN, featuring
Daddy's Little Helper and *Because of the Baby*
On sale July 2000

THE LAST TWO BACHELORS, featuring
Falling for Him and *Ending in Marriage*
On sale August 2000

Collect and enjoy each MIDNIGHT SONS story!

Available at your favorite retail outlet.

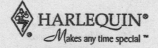